MW01596518

silly little monsters

Aly Welch

Writing Bloc

© **2020 Aly Welch**

All rights reserved. No part of this publication may be reproduced, stored in a retrieval system or transmited in any form or by any means, electronic, mechanical, photocopying, recording or otherwise without the prior permision of the publisher or in accordance with the provisions of the Copyright, Designs and Patents Act 1988 or under the terms of any licence permitting limited copying issued by the Copyright Licensing Angency.

Published by Writing Bloc

Editing: Cari Dubiel

Typesetting: Cari Dubiel

Cover Design: G.A. Finocchiaro & Aly Welch

ISBN-13: 9781087916446

Printed in USA

contents

For anyone who ever felt
alone or out of place

foreword

As I neared the completion of compiling this collection of stories, I struggled to think of a title to unify them. I found inspiration in a lyric from the Meg Myers song "Numb." She wrote this song about the music industry, but I know how it feels when people try to squeeze you into a box that does not fit.

I spoke my mind as a child and indulged in the sort of dark humor that has only recently become more mainstream. Peers and adults alike found me bothersome. I grew quieter, more withdrawn. I further compromised who I was in other ways instead of trusting my instincts—pleasing nobody, least of all myself. Music helped me channel my feelings into my work.

Where were unicorns like Meg Myers, Allie X, Lola Blanc, Tessa Violet, and Marina when I needed them in my youth?

In Marina especially, I found a kindred spirit. Her music helped me work through years of pent-up anger and sadness. She encouraged me to redefine success. I can't forgive or forget, but I found a path forward. Marina, like my favorite author Terry Pratchett, taught this tortoise how to fly.

Any similarities to actual people, places, or events in the stories ahead are as inevitable as they are coincidental. As Taylor in "Queen Bee" observes, people all too often play familiar roles in the same old dramas. I have certainly known more than a few preening bad boys like Vinny in "The Game." When I develop my characters, I too sometimes slip into the mix in unexpected ways. I even gave a piece of myself to Vinny, which may have altered the outcome of his story—for the better, I think.

You can imagine these stories taking place in a university town anywhere from California to the east coast. Tucson, Arizona may be a stretch, but a recurring campus hangout called the Cellar serves as a nod to my alma mater. I will let you decide whether all these tales exist in the same reality, or if different realities bleed into each other. Perhaps a character can take a seat in a dark corner of the Cellar in one universe, then step into another.

Some stories might have you questioning who the monster really is, or if there is even a monster in the story at all. In art, as in life, things are not always what they seem. Sometimes stories develop a life of their own and surprise even me, as was the case in "Resting Witch Face."

Though my work on *Silly Little Monsters* began in earnest a few years ago, "Triggered," "The Fang-over," and "Ghosted" were originally conceived as novels before I reimagined them as short stories. I wrote "The Game," "Queen Bee," "That Time of the Month," and "Resting Witch Face" expressly for this collection. The magical realism of "Alpha," which originally appeared in the Writing Bloc *Deception!* anthology, and its genre-bending sequel "Omega" serve as bookends. The order in which you read the stories does not matter, with one exception. "Omega" hits hardest if you save it for last.

I hope you find reading these stories as darkly amusing and cathartic as the experience of writing them was for me. See you on the other side.

alpha

"I'm so thrilled that Sara is finally bringing someone home to meet us," Mrs. Smith confided in her husband. The petite woman wore a pale green sleeveless dress that grazed her knees. A floral headscarf secured her light brown hair. She draped a freshly washed cream jacquard cloth over the mahogany table in the dining room.

"You sure I shouldn't get my shotgun?"

Mr. Smith sat on a tan recliner in the next room. He wore faded jeans and a rumpled tee. A baseball cap concealed his thinning brown hair, even though it annoyed his wife (or maybe *because* it annoyed her). He flipped through the channels, settling on a game show.

"Her friend is just joining us for a casual dinner, dear," Mrs. Smith reminded her husband as she adjusted the table cloth. "Save the 'scary dad' routine for their first real date. We don't want to chase a suitor off the first night."

Mrs. Smith walked into the kitchen. She

returned to the dining room with a round vase of daffodils that complemented the greens and yellows of her ensemble. Mrs. Smith set the floral arrangement down on the dining table. "Honestly, after what happened with Stacy's daughter, I was starting to worry about Sara."

"Hmm?"

"I'm surprised you didn't hear about it at work," Mrs. Smith replied as she rearranged the blooms, "her father working in accounting and all." She went back into the kitchen.

"You know I'm not much for water cooler talk unless the Packers are playing," Mr. Smith called out to her. "I hate gossip."

"Oh?"

Mrs. Smith possessed no such reservations. She came out of the kitchen with porcelain plates, yellow napkins, and silverware. "Well, a teacher caught Rachel in the bathroom with another girl," Mrs. Smith divulged as she set the table. Her tone suggested distaste, but her sparkling eyes betrayed an inner *this is better than reality TV* glee.

Mr. Smith looked away from the television and stared at his wife, raising a bushy eyebrow. "So…?"

Mrs. Smith walked under the archway of the partial wall to join him. He craned his neck to see the television.

"They were…," Mrs. Smith paused as though scandalized. She leaned over to whisper in her husband's ear. "They were…kissing."

Mr. Smith looked away from the television set again to meet his wife's eyes. "This is Jack Hansen's daughter, right? That Rachel?" The barest hint of a smile touched his lips. "The leggy brunette on Sara's softball team?"

"Yes. Rachel's a junior, too." Mrs. Smith narrowed her eyes. "Like our daughter."

"Who was the other girl?"

"Nobody we know." Mrs. Smith sighed and turned away.

A car pulled into the driveway.

"That's them." Mrs. Smith forced a smile. "Turn off the TV. I'll get the lemonade and glasses so we can enjoy a drink on the porch before dinner. There's about ten minutes left on the casserole." She returned to the kitchen.

Mr. Smith turned off the television and set down the remote. He pushed himself up from the chair. "I just hope he's not one of those effeminate pretty boys," he grumbled. Mr. Smith adjusted his baseball cap. He left the front door ajar for his wife as he stepped out into the warm spring air.

Mrs. Smith left the kitchen balancing a tray with a pitcher of lemonade and four glasses. She pushed the front door open with her free hand to join everyone outside.

Mr. Smith sat on the porch swing, holding his hat with one hand and scratching at his head with the other.

Mrs. Smith followed his eyes. She gasped, dropping the tray. The pitcher and glasses shattered on the sidewalk.

"Oops, party foul!" Sara knelt to pick up the broken pieces of glass. The pretty blonde wore a pink fitted tee and denim shorts. Her slim fingers deftly plucked at the glass, which she dropped into a decorative wastebasket by the swing.

Sara returned to the side of her guest. "Mom, this is Duke."

Duke stared at Mrs. Smith.

Mrs. Smith stared at Duke.

Duke towered over her. If not for his slouch, he appeared to be taller than Mr. Smith by nearly a foot. He had an impressive, tangled mane of black and auburn hair. What was most impressive about his hair was the way it covered most of his face and ran down his back. Mrs. Smith supposed it was fur rather than hair.

A pair of ram-like horns sat on either side of his large skull. His amber eyes glowed as if lit from within, reminding Mrs. Smith of a jack-o-lantern. He wore tattered clothing, and his feet were cloven.

Sara's hand disappeared into one of Duke's massive paws. Her other hand toyed with the fur on his muscular chest. She leaned against him, beaming at her mother.

Mrs. Smith stared down at her daughter's hand. She noticed the wickedly sharp claws on Duke's paw. Several moments passed before Mrs. Smith sputtered, "H...hello, Duke."

Duke opened his jaws wide, revealing a mouthful of yellow fangs. His breath stank as he grunted in greeting. Duke lumbered off to investigate the foliage in the yard. He stopped to look in Mrs. Smith's direction and wag his short deer-like tail.

"He has a tail," Mrs. Smith said to nobody in particular, her fingers fiddling with a strand of pearls at her throat. She tilted her head as she watched Duke tear through her garden, crushing daffodils.

He stopped to hurl a large stone at Sara. Duke beat his gargantuan chest and whooped.

Sara ducked, grinning.

"Aww. See how much he likes me? Johnny only ever threw sand and pebbles."

"That was in kindergarten," Mrs. Smith said. "But it's not okay at any age."

Sara's blue eyes widened with surprise. "Really? You didn't mind back then. Even thought it was cute."

Mrs. Smith frowned. She saw Duke stop circling the yard to sniff the trunk of a maple tree. Her eyebrows rose when she heard a noise that sounded suspiciously like a zipper.

"See, he feels right at home already!"

Sara clapped her hands together with delight.

"Did he...did he just mark the tree?" Mrs. Smith turned to her husband.

Mr. Smith was still staring straight ahead, his eyes glazed over.

"You always told me to find a big, strong Alpha," Sara reasoned. "But don't worry. He knows Dad is the man of the house."

Duke ran to her father on all fours. Mr. Smith jumped up and dropped his hat. As Duke acquainted himself with the man of the house's thigh, Mr. Smith's gaze darted from Duke to his wife to his daughter. His eyes were no longer glazed over, but wide and bulging.

Mrs. Smith raised a hand to her mouth, her own eyes just as wide as she turned to her daughter.

"Stop that." Sara tapped Duke on the head. He disentangled himself from Mr. Smith and rose to his full height. Then he tugged on Sara's flaxen ponytail, hard.

"No!" she said sharply, tapping the bridge of his nose.

Duke whimpered, his lower lip jutting out.

"It's okay," Sara consoled him, stroking his downy cheek. "Is dinner ready yet?" she asked her mother. "Duke is starving." Sara opened the front door and walked inside.

Duke followed her.

Mrs. Smith heard a thump and a crash as a table lamp fell to the floor. She winced.

Mr. Smith knelt down to retrieve his hat. "Are we really gonna allow that thing in our house?" He rose, trying to smooth his disheveled hair as he put his hat back on.

"Sara likes it…er, him," Mrs. Smith replied. "We should give him a chance. My father didn't care for you much, either," she added, turning to go inside. "Not until he got to know you better."

"I never violated hi…" Mr. Smith paused, scowling. "I never got into his personal space," he grumbled under his breath as he followed his wife into the house.

"Duke won't need these," Sara said as she took the utensils from his napkin and returned them to the kitchen. She came back with a stack of paper towels, which she set on the table in front of Duke.

Duke sat hunched over in his chair. His knees were too high to fit comfortably beneath the mahogany table. Mrs. Smith worried the chair would shatter under his considerable weight, but for now it held.

"Soup or salad?" she asked.

"Soup," Sara answered for him. "Duke doesn't like rabbit food. He's a meat and potatoes kind of guy."

"He's not a 'guy' at all," Mr. Smith muttered. He took his seat at the head of the table.

Mrs. Smith glared at her husband.

Sara followed her mother into the kitchen. After a quiet but terse conversation, she came out with a bowl of salad that she set down on the table. Mrs. Smith carried a pot of soup. She ladled some of the soup into Duke's bowl.

Duke leaned forward, grunting as he sniffed the soup, his expression wary. He buried his face in the bowl, slurping noisily. Mrs. Smith ladled some more soup for Duke before handing the pot to Mr. Smith.

Sara and Mrs. Smith served themselves salad.

Duke finished the rest of his soup. He whined, glancing at the empty bowl, then turned toward the kitchen. He sniffed the air and harrumphed impatiently.

Mr. Smith glared in his general direction.

Sara and Mrs. Smith picked at their salads.

"So, how was work today, Da-?" A beeping sound in the kitchen interrupted Sara.

Mrs. Smith rose to retrieve her casserole from the oven. She returned, wearing a kitchen mitt and holding a pan and spatula to serve everyone. Once she finished, Mrs. Smith looked at Duke.

Duke looked at Mrs. Smith, who gave him a nod of encouragement. Then he looked at the casserole. His lip rose into a sneer, and he stuck a paw in the dish. As he held the paw over his head, a gooey bit of casserole fell into his mouth. His eyes grew wide.

Then he rose with a roar and proceeded to throw bits of casserole at everyone.

"That is it!" Mr. Smith yelled, rising from his seat. "Get out of my house!" he bellowed.

Duke stopped throwing bits of casserole and stared at Mr. Smith, his nostrils flaring. Then he leaped over the table, baring his fangs as he snarled.

Mr. Smith backed away, his hands raised.

Duke turned to Sara, lifted her from her seat, and flung her over his shoulder. Using his head as a battering ram, he tore into the living room and barreled right through a wall, leaving behind a Duke-and-Sara-shaped hole.

"He's quite the rugged brute, isn't he?" Mrs. Smith said as she held a hand to her chest.

"That brute just put a damn hole in our house!" Mr. Smith yelled.

Mrs. Smith offered a meek smile as she turned to her husband.

"Boys will be boys...?"

Duke set Sara down on the grass in a large field a few blocks from her home. She touched her backside, wincing. Duke whimpered an apology.

"Just a little tender. I've experienced worse in softball," Sara reassured him. She crossed the street to a light blue Prius. Sara opened the trunk and retrieved something wrapped in butcher paper. She returned to Duke, handing him a large shank of raw meat. He held it between his teeth and bowed his head low so she could scratch behind one of his horns. Then he ran on all fours across the field, heading for a line of dense trees.

Sara crossed the street and opened the passenger door of the Prius.

"Oh my god. He is amazing! Where did you find him?" Rachel asked from the back seat. She sat with an arm draped around a voluptuous redhead.

"Okay," Sara began. "So, you know all those stories about some scary monster attacking anyone who parks up the hill at Lookout Point?" Sara asked. "Well, Duke's the monster. We ran into him last week. Like, literally. Did Chris show you the dent in his front bumper?" The girls shook their heads.

"Anyway, we got out of the car because we thought we hit a person. He was fine, but all sorts of embarrassed and totally sweet. That's when I had the idea."

"It'll definitely soften the blow when your parents meet Captain Guyliner," laughed the redhead, Emily.

Sara turned to ruffle the driver's dark shaggy hair.

"Hey, wanna try that new vegan place before my gig? They have ethically raised burgers, too," Chris assured Sara. He started the car and drove away, revealing several band decals and a "coexist" sticker on the rear window of the Prius.

Somewhere in the woods, Duke released a triumphant howl. He settled into his cave to gnaw on the bone from the shank of raw meat Sara had gifted him.

triggered

"C'mon, baby girl," Nurse Jackson cajoled Julia Hernandez. "Be good and take your medicine." Though the stocky woman cut an imposing figure in her slate blue scrubs, affection softened her dark eyes as she gazed at the petite girl.

Julia wore a white tee shirt and gray sweatpants. Her messy reddish-brown curls fell from a haphazard ponytail, but her brown eyes remained sharp and alert. "Okay," she said, accepting two small paper cups from the nurse's outstretched hand. One cup contained a small pill, the other, water. "But only because you asked nicely." She grinned, her cheeks dimpling.

"And because you know I'll lay your ass out if you give me a hard time," Nurse Jackson said.

Julia rolled her eyes, still grinning. She made a dramatic show of putting the pill in her mouth before taking a sip of water. Then she stuck her tongue out for Nurse Jackson to confirm she had indeed swallowed the pill.

Nurse Jackson raised an eyebrow. She placed her thumb and index finger on either cheek to force Julia's mouth open and pluck the pill from between her teeth and lower lip.

"Child…"

Julia shrugged with a rueful *can't blame a girl for trying* smirk as she took the pill back from Nurse Jackson. This time, she swallowed.

"You've got your session with Dr. Harper in an hour," Nurse Jackson reminded Julia as she left the room. The heavy door slammed shut behind her.

Julia sensed sadness and something else she could not quite identify in the nurse's wake.

Trepidation, perhaps?

Nurse Jackson had something weighing on her mind, that much was certain, but it did not mean it had anything to do with Julia. Still, she wondered as she sat on her cot and gazed out the window. Sunshine streamed in between the bars. The warmth felt heavenly in her otherwise cool room. Sighing, Julia laid down with her hands behind her head to stare at the ceiling.

"Okay, Julia," Dr. Harper said, adjusting his glasses. "I know that we've talked about this before, but I want you to walk me through the events that led to your placement in our care. Only this time, I want you to dive deeper into the emotions. Maybe you can consider the events from your uncle's point of view."

"Seriously?" Julia asked, her tone dark.

Dr. Harper nodded, apprehension flashing in his

watery blue eyes. His sandy brown hair looked more disheveled than usual. Julia knew she could put the young psychologist at ease if she chose, but she fixed him with a cool stare instead.

"Well, first of all, I was not 'placed' in your care. I was imprisoned here against my will because my uncle didn't want to be inconvenienced by his sister's poor life choices."

"This isn't a prison," Dr. Harper said with a weary sigh.

"Really?" Julia said. "That's not the impression I got from the bars on my window."

"Tell me more about your relationship with your uncle."

"I never met Uncle Tomas until after the car accident. His wife's not so bad. Emilia takes care of me. She makes the best carne asada. You see, the trick to keeping it tender is that you have to-"

"I asked about your uncle," Dr. Harper reminded her gently.

Julia scowled. "Uncle Tomas just ignores me. Except when he gets on my case for being anything less than perfect. I bet he was the same way with my mom. She always said he was too bossy and over-protective, just like their father."

Julia's eyes took on a faraway look.

"One night, I couldn't sleep, so I went down-stairs. He was sitting in his chair in the family room, crying. He wasn't making any noise, not really, but I could see the wetness on his cheeks. He had pictures in his lap, of him and my mom when they were little. I didn't say anything, just put my hand on his shoul-der. He went still for a while. I think he almost fell asleep, but then he jumped up and started calling me names."

Julia fell silent.

Her eyes filled with tears.

"What sort of names?" Dr. Harper asked. He waited.

"Bruja," Julia said at last. "That's what he called me."

Bruja.

A young woman with green eyes and long red hair sat in the office next to Dr. Harper's, a few tears rolling down her face. An older woman wearing a lab coat peered at her, taking notes as she spoke. "She felt so lost," the redhead said. "Not only can I hear her thoughts, but I can feel her loneliness gnawing at my insides. Please don't make me listen anymore. You have what you need."

"Your cousins told your aunt Emilia you sat by yourself at lunch every day," Dr. Harper said, his voice soft. "You weren't making any friends. In fact, you seemed intent on being as repellant to others as possible. You talked back to teachers, didn't do your work. She was worried."

"Maybe," Julia said, wiping a single tear from her cheek. "But Uncle Tomas just thinks I'm evil." Her defiant glare returned. "I don't see the point of this. If anyone's crazy, it's him. Can I go back to my cell?"

"The bars are only there for your safety," Dr. Harper said with another heavy sigh. He pressed a buzzer on his desk.

A different nurse led Julia back to her room.

"You have a visitor," Nurse Jackson said later that day.

Julia looked up from the television in the common area with a scowl. "It's my personal time," she complained.

"Baby girl, if it was up to me, you'd get to keep watching your stories," Nurse Jackson replied, "but it ain't, so let's get goin'."

Julia rose from her chair, looking pensive. Nurse Jackson's sour demeanor suggested the visitor was her uncle. When he'd first had Julia institutionalized, his gruff manner had not made the best impression .

Maybe Aunt Emilia talked him into taking me home.

Julia doubted it. She liked the nurses and even that dopey Dr. Harper more than her uncle. But she desired her freedom more.

"You're not my uncle Tomas," Julia said as Nurse Jackson ushered her into the office.

"Thank goodness for that," said a slim woman dressed in a lab coat over a pink tee shirt and jeans. She had a chin-length blond bob and a wide smile. Her blue eyes twinkled as she reached out to shake Julia's hand. "I'm Dr. Martin."

Julia stared at her hand without taking it. "What happened to Dr. Harper?" she asked.

"Nothing," Dr. Martin said. "Your uncle approved a transfer. I'll be caring for you at a different facility. I think you'll find it much more..." The doctor paused as she regarded the sterile office with its barren white walls and sparse furnishing. "Inviting," she finished.

Her warmth felt genuine, but Julia sensed a secret behind the doctor's smile. She looked at Nurse Jackson, whose face gave away nothing.

Julia turned back to Dr. Martin.

"When do we leave?"

"Take care of yourself, baby girl," Nurse Jackson said.

Julia felt a sudden compulsion to hug the nurse. The affectionate gesture surprised the both of them. "Go on now," Nurse Jackson added gruffly as she untangled herself from Julia.

Julia picked up her small duffel bag and walked to a gray sedan. A redhead sat up front.

Guess it's too late to call shotgun, Julia thought.

Or maybe she said it aloud, because the redhead offered a look of apology when Julia sat down in the backseat of the car. She felt her forehead wrinkle in apprehension as she regarded the redhead, but she sensed nothing from the woman but friendly curiosity.

"Julia, this is Madison. She's part of my team at Shady Glen," Dr. Martin said as she sat down in the driver's seat. She started the car and began to back out of the parking spot. Julia looked up at the entrance, but Nurse Jackson had already gone back inside.

"Shady Glen?" Julia's eyes returned to Dr. Martin, narrowing with distrust.

"Yes," Dr. Martin said. "We thought it best to stick with a name that didn't reveal too much of our purpose to outsiders."

Julia thought it sounded a bit, well, shady, but

didn't say anything else. Her head rose sharply when Madison chuckled. She caught a glimpse of Dr. Martin giving the redhead a pointed look. Madison clammed up for the rest of the drive.

Dr. Martin slowed down as they reached a small rural road framed by trees on either side. Eventually the thick forest parted to reveal a large manicured lawn and sprawling estate; no fencing surrounded the grounds that Julia could see, but a couple of large black dogs lounged in the grass, their tongues lolling over massive jaws.

"There's invisible fencing," Madison said. "Echo and India have collars that…well, it's just a little zap, if they stray past the fencing."

"Will I have to wear a collar?" Julia asked, scowling.

"No," Dr. Martin said. "We're not worried about you running away." She winked at Madison. "That's why we have the dogs."

Julia could not tell if she was joking.

"We have tennis courts and a basketball court in back," Dr. Martin said as they exited the sedan. "That's where the others are so you can get settled before introductions."

Julia followed Dr. Martin and Madison to the front door of the manor. "Tennis courts, huh? Fancy."

"You'll find Shady Glen is quite different from your prior… home away from home," Dr. Martin said. "Madison will show you to your room. I have some paperwork to complete."

Madison opened the door to a room with

wooden blinds, the slats open to allow sunlight to stream in through windows without bars.

"I have a roommate?" Julia asked when she saw the bunk bed. The top bunk was unmade and covered with clothing.

"Kaylie. She can be, well...uhm." Madison paused. "I'm sure you'll get along fine," she finished, flashing a grin. "Oh, Dr. Martin wants you to wear this. It's just for today." Madison removed a name tag from her pocket.

After Julia set down her bag, she walked to the window to gaze outside. Seeing nothing obstructing it, she was about to slide it open, but someone knocked on the door. Madison was back.

"Everyone's heading to the dining room," Madison told her. "Oh, and don't forget your name tag."

Julia made a face. She peeled the name tag off the strip of paper and affixed it to the front of her shirt. Following Madison down the hall, Julia nearly bumped into a taller boy with a light tan and brown hair and eyes.

He looked at her, then down at her name tag. "Hola, Hulia."

"Hello, Hoe," Julia replied after glancing at his nametag.

Joe ducked his head, flashing a sheepish grin.

"Smooth," Madison said. "Let's go." She led them into the dining room. "We like to keep things informal around here," Madison explained. She took a seat at one end of a long dining table. Dr. Martin already sat on the other end.

Joe sat down between a boy with pale skin and shaggy black hair that fell into his heavily lined eyes and a sullen-looking girl with shoulder-length waves that transitioned in color from pink to purple to aqua. Her name tag said "Kaylie."

Julia sat across from Kaylie. Two other boys sat on Julia's side. One boy had messy red hair, green eyes, and freckles across his nose. The other had glasses, black cornrows, and a relaxed grin.

"Why don't we begin with everyone introducing themselves to Julia so she can get to know all of you," Dr. Martin said.

"I'm Trevor." The boy with cornrows fixed his amiable gaze on Julia. "I'm from Philly. My parents were worried my gift might attract the wrong attention, so they sent me here."

Julia had never heard someone refer to their mental illness as a gift before, but Trevor did not strike her as mentally ill, either. Julia looked at Dr. Martin, confused.

"Trevor, can you give Julia a demonstration?"

Trevor smiled but he didn't do anything. Julia saw movement out the corner of her eye. Her eyes widened as a clipboard and pencil in front of Dr. Martin rose and flew across the table into Trevor's hands. "Telekinesis," he said.

"I'm Matthew," the redhead began before Julia could ask any questions. "You already noticed the family resemblance." He grinned at Madison. "I'm a telepath, too."

Telepath.

Too...?

Julia remembered Madison's strange behavior in the car. She glared at her.

"Sorry." Madison smiled. "We try hard to respect

personal boundaries and the privacy of others, but our gift can be hard to control. Ethics are a big part of what Dr. Martin's staff teaches here at Shady Glen. You'll meet them tomorrow."

"On that note," Dr. Martin interrupted her, "Chris will not be able to demonstrate his gift, but he did know you were coming." The pale boy glanced in Julia's direction through his mop of dark hair, but remained silent. "Precognition can be a tricky gift to navigate. There are more than just ethical concerns to worry about."

Up until that point, Joe had been leaning back in his chair with his eyes closed, but now he sat up straight and stared at Julia. "Your bed is a mess." His lips spread into a wide grin. "You have lacy black underwear with cherries on it. Nice."

Kaylie backhanded him in his chest, hard. "That's my bunk, you ass!"

Joe coughed, but he was laughing. Julia felt Kaylie's anger as if it was her own, roiling in her stomach. Her forehead became hot. The warmth spread from her face down to her neck, shoulders, and arms into her hands.

"Dr. Martin?" Trevor rested his hand on Julia's shoulder.

"Madison, take Kaylie upstairs. Joe, go to my office. Keep an eye on him," Dr. Martin ordered Trevor and Jackson.

"What can Kaylie do?" Julia asked after the room emptied. She no longer felt feverish.

"Let's just say Joe is lucky she didn't use an open palm," Dr. Martin replied. "He can't touch anything in his astral state, but snooping remains a concern."

"This isn't a mental institution, is it?"

"I'll explain later. Get some rest." Dr. Martin ushered her out of the room.

"Makes you wish you were back in the nuthouse, doesn't it?" Kaylie asked from the top bunk when Julia walked in.

"I do miss the rubber walls." Julia looked around the room. Unlike the plain white walls of the hospital, these were painted a pleasant shade of blue. A dresser sat across from the bunk bed. Julia dumped the contents of her bag into an empty drawer, sensing Kaylie's eyes on her back.

"So, what's your gift?" Kaylie asked.

"Don't have one." Julia shrugged.

"Whatever." Kaylie rolled over and closed her eyes.

"You've figured out this place isn't a mental institution." Dr. Martin grinned as Julia sat down with a plate of spaghetti for dinner. "What Shady Glen really does is provide education to gifted children. Some choose to come here. Others, like you and Kaylie, get mistaken for mentally ill."

"Kaylie really is crazy, though," Joe interrupted.

Dr. Martin silenced him with a look. "Julia, you are what's known as a power empath," she continued. "You can absorb other people's feelings and project your own. You can even enhance the gifts of others."

"So, what? She's like some sort of human battery?" Kaylie's voice oozed with disdain. "Lamest superpower ever."

"Actually," Dr. Martin said as she adjusted her glasses. "Julia is stronger than you realize. Imagine the strength it requires to maintain her gift even as she empowers those around her. You will all be stronger for being in her presence."

"I think Julia's less like a human battery, and more like a quartz crystal," Matthew stated. Kaylie rolled her eyes. "Think about it," he continued. "Crystals amplify psychic ability and improve focus. Maybe Julia can, too."

"Yeah, well, I can't wear her around my neck," Kaylie said. Joe snickered. Madison gave him a look of disgust.

"I don't have superpowers," Julia said, ignoring them.

"Not superpowers, just a less common gift," Dr. Martin. "We still have so much to learn. Full disclosure, I'm studying you, but mostly our goal is teaching you how to use your gift wisely."

"And then you enlist us in some sort of psyops, right? For, like, the military? Or the CIA, or something? I mean, this is government, right? It has to be."

"Some students get unique job opportunities." Dr. Martin's smile remained coy. "Others lead normal lives as civilians."

"I bet you'd be great at something like hostage negotiations," Trevor told Julia. "You can calm people down, get the bad guy to trust you."

She could not help but return his grin.

"Still doesn't look like anything special to me," Kaylie mumbled.

Julia ignored her and began to eat.

Chris remained quiet during dinner, and Kaylie went back to their room, but Julia moved into the family room with the others to play cards and talk. She learned more about Trevor, Matthew, and Madison while Joe sat back and listened. Julia suspected his silence was out of character. She could not get a read on him.

Joe stopped Julia in the hall later. "I know that I didn't make the best first impression, but there's some things about Shady Glen you should know. Think you can stay up awhile, until one? We can meet up in the family room."

Though her first impulse was to decline his invitation, Julia sensed such an urgency in his voice that she nodded instead.

"So, what's up?"

Joe looked up at Julia with an impish smirk. He stretched out in the chair, resting his feet on an ottoman and his hands behind his head. "I didn't think you'd come. Has anyone ever told you that your dimples are adorable?"

"No, never." Julia turned to leave.

Joe's laconic grin faded as he straightened. "Wait. I don't know who Dr. Martin works for, but she isn't government. I overheard her on the phone. Something's happening. Soon. I think you can help me get us out of here before it does."

"Us?" Julia sat across from Joe on the sofa.

"Madison is one of hers. That means Matthew is, too. If Chris has picked up on anything, he hasn't ratted me out, but…no. I'm pretty sure Trevor's all in. Kaylie's nuts. It's just you and me, kiddo."

Julia made a face. "I only just got here, and like you said, you haven't made the best first impression. How do I know you're not just messing with me."

Joe shrugged. "There's nothing I can do or say to make you trust me, but do you really think this place is on the up and up? I mean, you've seen all the security cameras, right?"

"The place I came from had cameras, too."

Joe rolled his eyes. "Because it's a mental institute. This is supposed to be a school. You know of any schools with high tech security and massive guard dogs? Even if Dr. Martin…no, *especially* if Dr. Martin works for the government, you'll never have your freedom again. No way are they gonna let any of us walk out of here to live a normal civilian life."

If Joe was right, Julia doubted they'd get very far tonight either, but they might be in even worse trouble tomorrow if Dr. Martin reviewed the security footage. She sighed. "So, what do you want me to do?"

"Think you can make the dogs go to sleep?"

Julia's eyes widened.

"Just a joke," Joe reassured her. "I slipped something into their food. They should be out cold for the night, but I still need a code to shut down the security system. I think it's written in a notebook that Dr. Martin keeps in her nightstand. It's too risky to sneak into her room, but if Dr. Martin is right about you, you can help me look another way. I've been close to opening the notebook on my own. If we combine powers, maybe I can do it."

"How do we combine powers?" Her eyes narrowed.

"Skin on skin contact."

When Julia rose to leave, Joe stood and held out his hands.

"Not like that," he said. "Maybe just hold my hand?"

Julia remained distrustful but sat. Joe sat beside her and held out his hand. She took it. To her relief, his hand felt soft and dry instead of wet and clammy like she worried. Joe leaned back, closing his eyes.

Julia waited.

After several tense moments, Joe opened his eyes. "5552323. 5552323. Remember that. Let's go!" He stood.

"What about my things?"

"No time." Joe reclaimed Julia's hand. "I've got money. You can buy new things." He led her to the front hall. Joe opened a panel beside the door to punch in the numbers.

"VERBAL AUTHENTICATION REQUIRED," boomed a robotic voice.

"Shit!"

"VERBAL AUTHENTICATION DENIED."

An alarm blared, and a light in every room flashed green and red. Joe threw open the front door, pulling Julia along after him.

"They'll be coming any minute! Hurry!"

"Who's they?" Julia asked, but her voice was drowned out by the shrill bleeps and lower- pitched honks of the alarm. They raced down the driveway to the road. The alarm was no longer deafening, but now Julia heard a low growl.

Joe turned to face the source. His eyes widened as a large dog leapt at him and knocked him to the ground. Julia turned to run, but something crashed into her.

Not a dog, but a person.

"Hold my hand!"

Julia stared dumbfounded at a fully clothed Kaylie, but she snapped to attention and took the girl's outstretched hand. Kaylie held her free hand up in the direction of the dog. Julia's eyes widened as a ball of fire roared to life and soared from Kaylie's hand to strike the dog in its side. The dog released Joe's throat, howling in pain as it rolled and thrashed on the grass to snuff out the flames.

Trevor and Chris arrived next, also clothed. Trevor knelt beside Joe's motionless body. "I'd take his pulse, but..." He gestured at the ruins of Joe's throat.

Julia looked away, retching.

"You didn't mention this part," Kaylie told Chris as she helped Julia to her feet.

"We gotta go," Trevor said. "Dr. Martin was working on the alarm and barking orders at Madison, but they'll be here any minute, with backup. Is your guy on the outside on the way?"

"She's coming."

Kaylie's eyes widened as she stared over Trevor's shoulder.

"Move!"

They started to run as the other dog raced toward them. It leapt for Julia as they reached the road, but then it fell with a yelp. It continued to whimper, kicking and clawing at the collar around its throat.

An unmarked van pulled up to the curb. Kaylie ushered the others into the back before she climbed into the front passenger seat.

"Where's the fifth?" a familiar voice asked.

"Didn't make it," Kaylie told her.

Julia stared up at the driver in wonder. Nurse Jackson winked at Julia's reflection in the rearview mirror. Julia turned back to Kaylie. "Who are you people?"

"Not government," Kaylie told Julia, "but neither is Dr. Martin. Joe was right about that. He approached me first, but I couldn't blow my cover. I knew the doctor was recruiting for foreign enemies, but I still needed an extraction plan for Chris and Trevor. Chris came to me with a vision of Joe providing a distraction, but he left out certain key details."

She glared at Chris. He shrugged, his expression mild.

"Joe was a creep, but he could shield his thoughts from the telepaths, when he wanted to, and his abilities would have been useful to us," Kaylie continued.

"I still don't understand who you are," Julia said.

"We're rogue agents, like Dr. Martin. But we try to use our powers to help people instead. Constance...Nurse Jackson likes to say we tend to the edges."

"How do I know I can trust you?"

"You may not be a telepath like Madison or Matthew, but you have good instincts. What do they tell you?"

Julia looked at the others in turn. Trevor met

her eyes with an encouraging smile. Julia turned back to Kaylie. "My instincts are telling me that your superpower is way cooler than mine, but I think I can still help."

"Don't underestimate yourself. Constance never did."

Nurse Jackson turned to Julia with a warm smile. "Welcome to the family, baby girl."

that time of the month

Nicole Farkas reclined against the fluffy pillows on her bed as she slogged through a novel assigned in her honors English class. She had reached the conclusion that the moors of England were far more interesting when roamed by devilish dogs and clever detectives than by angsty lovers who did not need the stars to cross for their overblown romance to falter.

"Nobody cares, Cathy. You live in the middle of nowhere," Nicole muttered to herself, fighting an urge to throw the book across the room.

Outside, the wind howled, and tree branches hit the sides of the two-story home. Nicole did not notice the tapping at her window at first. After a minute, the tapping heightened in intensity. Nicole glanced up and gasped. She leapt from the bed, the book falling to the floor.

Nicole opened the window. A disheveled boy with dirty blond hair and green eyes crawled inside.

"It's after eight. You told me your parents were

going to some work thing, remember?" Ben Wilson said. He walked to Nicole's bed and sat down.

Nicole laughed, sitting beside him. "Yeah, I figured you'd text me once you got here, and I'd let you in through the front door like a normal person."

"What would your neighbors say?"

"I think a boy climbing up the side of my house on a stormy night is a little more conspicuous than coming to the front door, don't you?" Nicole told him.

"Hey, whatcha reading?" Ben asked, leaning over to pick the book up off the floor. "A love story?"

"I love hating on it." Nicole reached over Ben to take the book from his hand. Ben smelled fresh and clean, soapy with a hint of sandalwood, like the gray oversized hoodie she'd claimed from him as her own. Nicole set the book down on her nightstand.

When Nicole straightened back up, Ben gave her a coy smile. "Your hair smells nice," he said, tucking a stray sun-kissed strand behind Nicole's ear.

Nicole kissed Ben on the lips, holding either side of his face. After his initial surprise, he kissed back. Ben tangled his hands in her light golden-brown waves.

Nicole felt a strange ache in her jaw. She ignored it as the kiss deepened. Her skin began to tingle, but not with the excited anticipation she was used to; instead, it almost burned, and not with pleasure.

Now Nicole pulled away to take a breath.

Ben gazed at her with concern. "You okay? We can slow down."

"No, I'm fine," Nicole reassured him. "I just have, like, a toothache or something." She put her hands on his shoulders and leaned in for another kiss, but she pressed her lips against his harder than she intended.

This time Ben pulled away. "Easy, Nikki."

"Sorry." Nicole looked away and put her hands in her lap, contrite.

Ben kissed her cheek, then touched her other cheek, turning her to face him as he kissed her on the lips. The jaw pain and burning sensation under her skin seemed to subside as Nicole lost herself in the kiss, eager to recapture the mood.

Outside, the storm waned. The clouds parted to reveal the full moon, large and bright. Nicole's fingers curled into claws as she grasped Ben's chest. She tossed her head back and howled with pain. The last thing Nicole saw was Ben's frightened face staring back at her, his green eyes reflecting something that no longer resembled a teenage girl.

Nicole awoke in a tangle of torn sheets, naked and alone. She saw a feather out of the corner of her eye and plucked it from her hair. More feathers covered the bed and the floor, strewn around the remains of ruined pillows.

Ben.

Nicole remembered seeing the terror in his eyes before she blacked out. There was no sign of him in her room. But she didn't see any blood either, and that was a good sign.

Right?

Nicole stood up and reached for a plush green bathrobe that hung from a hook over her bedroom door. Slipping into the robe, she stepped out of her room into the hallway.

Nicole heard her parents moving downstairs with surprising clarity. Not just the banging of pots and pans in the kitchen, but the shuffle of feet across carpet in the living room and the rustle of fabric against fabric.

The tantalizing smell of bacon wafted up the stairs from the kitchen, but Nicole tiptoed down the hall into the bathroom. She closed the door with only the faintest of clicks, feeling grateful her parents did not share her newly heightened senses. Nicole regarded her reflection in the mirror. Bits of leaves and twigs accented her tangled hair. She shrugged off her robe to inspect her pale skin, dirty but unscathed.

After untangling the forest debris from her hair, Nicole took a shower. She scrubbed dirt from her skin until she was red and blotchy as she replayed the events of last night and this morning. Her suspicions about herself were at odds with reality as she knew it, but the bigger concern was Ben and his well-being. Her stomach growled as she turned off the water and towel-dried her hair.

Another good sign?

Nicole hoped so. The thought of hurting Ben, or worse, made her heart ache. She looked in the mirror as she slid the bathrobe back on. Her lips were pursed with tension and her dark eyes appeared almost haunted. She patted her cheeks until the color returned to her face, and her eyes brightened. Satisfied with her appearance, she went to her room to get dressed.

Hungry for breakfast, Nicole tried to slink past the living room on her way to the kitchen, but her stomach betrayed her when it rumbled at the smell of bacon. She winced.

"Nicole, can you come in here?" Mrs. Farkas said.

Nicole took a long deep breath before she turned around to face her parents. Mr. and Mrs. Farkas sat on the couch, their faces kind, if concerned.

Did they not know Ben had come inside through her window last night? Or that her bed was shredded?

Nicole maintained a neutral expression as she sat across from her parents in a plush armchair.

Mr. and Mrs. Farkas looked at each other. Mr. Farkas gave a sort of nod. Mrs. Farkas began to speak. "In light of whatever happened last night, I think we have some things we need to discuss," she said.

"We do?" Nicole hoped her mother didn't notice the tremor in her voice.

"We do," Mrs. Farkas said. "Your father and I know you were gone last night, and we saw the condition that you left your room in. I think it's time we had a little talk. I was hoping it wouldn't come to this, but you're obviously going through some very big changes and, well, it's time to stop avoiding the conversation."

Nicole's eyes widened. "But we already had *the talk*. When I was, like, nine."

"No, not *that* talk. Not really. There's something else we need to explain to you, now that you're of age," Mrs. Farkas continued.

"Oh, please no," Nicole whimpered.

"Would it make you feel better if I left the room

while you discuss this?" her father asked, beginning to rise.

"Yes!" Nicole said.

"No," said her mother, patting his knee. "You're a part of this story, too," she told him. He gave a rueful nod, sinking back into the sofa.

Nicole raised an eyebrow.

"Can *I* leave the room?"

"We never told you the story of our honeymoon," Mrs. Farkas said, ignoring Nicole's discomfort. She gazed out the window behind the couch, a dreamy look on her face as she talked. "We were backpacking across Europe. We began in England and ended in Hungary, where your father's family comes from."

"I don't get what any of this has to do with me," Nicole interrupted.

"I'm getting to that," her mother said.

"We were leaving a café in St. Andrews when she approached us," Mr. Farkas chimed in. Mrs. Farkas gave him a sharp glance but let him speak. "A strange old beggar woman. She asked us for food, but we were tired and wanted to go back to the hostel, so your mother offered her some money instead. The woman took great offense. It was only then I noticed her jewelry: so many rings and necklaces with giant baubles. Nothing worth much, I'm sure. Just costume jewelry. I suppose she was a gypsy?"

"Dad, I don't think you're supposed to ca-"

Mrs. Farkas continued where Mr. Farkas had left off. "She began to sway and moan, and she told us our firstborn would turn into a wolf by the light of the first full moon after her eighteenth birthday. Of course, we didn't believe her. It all seemed so cliché, and a bit of an overreaction to a simple misunderstanding, if I'm being perfectly honest."

Nicole knitted her brows but remained silent.

"I must admit her words came back to me after you were born, but your father reminded me she had a fifty percent chance of being right about you being a girl. After that, I forgot all about the curse until we came home last night."

"When we pulled into the driveway, we noticed your bedroom window was wide open," Mr. Farkas said. "We weren't too worried at first, but when we went upstairs to your room, you were gone, and your bed was a mess. Like a wild animal had torn it apart. All those feathers."

"So many feathers," Mrs. Farkas agreed, her eyes distant.

"We couldn't call anyone," Mr. Farkas said. "What would we even say?"

"All we could do was wait and hope you would come home safely. I think we may have dozed off sometime before sunrise. When we woke up and took another look in your room, you were curled up asleep," Mrs. Farkas explained.

Nicole felt her cheeks flush.

"All your…girl parts…were covered," her father assured her.

Now Nicole felt warm to the tips of her ears.

"You don't seem that surprised," Mrs. Farkas observed. She leaned forward as she peered into Nicole's eyes. "Do you remember what happened to you? Anything at all?"

Nicole looked away. "I don't think anything can surprise me after last night," she replied. "I remember reading my book. It was stormy outside. Then the clouds parted, and I saw the moon, and...I dunno. My jaw started to ache. I felt this horrible pain, like I wanted to crawl out of my skin. Then I woke up."

It was not a lie. Not exactly.

"We made some calls while you were sleeping. Unfortunately, we don't know anyone who knows how to break curses or treat lycanthropy," Mr. Farkas said, his tone so mild he may as well have been discussing the common cold. "But I do have a friend at the city zoo. I asked him some hypothetical questions about the sort of equipment one would need to rescue large predators. Cages, tranquilizers, that sort of thing."

"You're gonna lock me up in a cage?" Nicole squeaked.

Perhaps she should feel relieved euthanasia was not on the table, assuming her parents already considered that option and ruled it out, but the thought of being confined like a wild animal horrified Nicole.

"Only when there's a full moon," Mrs. Farkas clarified. "It's for your own safety until we find a better solution. You're attending the local university next fall anyway, and the basement's not so bad now that it's finished. We can put a TV down there for you and everything." She turned to Mr. Farkas. "I've read that dogs enjoy watching nature programs."

"Are you sure Nicole wouldn't find it too stimulating when she's...you know?" Mr. Farkas asked his wife. He bared his teeth and curved his fingers into claws.

Nicole stared at her parents, aghast. She had not

felt this embarrassed since the time her dad shouted a question about tampon brands at the grocery store. "I...I'm sorry," she said. "This is all too much. Is there any reason why I can't leave the house? Go for a walk, maybe, to clear my head?"

Her parents exchanged a look.

"I don't see why not," Mr. Farkas said.

"But eat something before you go," Mrs. Farkas said. "I can fry up some more eggs and bacon for you."

Nicole wanted to decline, but her stomach rumbled noisily.

"Guess your first hunt didn't go so well," Mr. Farkas said, smiling. "No worries. I'll make arrangements with a local butcher for next time."

Nicole offered a weak smile.

Upstairs in her room, Nicole slipped on Ben's hoodie. She breathed in his residual scent deeply. Tears welled up in her eyes. She would have heard something by now if something had happened to him, wouldn't she?

Nicole took the phone out of her pocket. Ben still had not read her text message. She considered dialing, but put the phone back in her pocket instead. Nicole put on a pair of sneakers. She pulled her wet hair into a messy ponytail.

Outside, the air felt warm and inviting. Birds chirped and bees buzzed around flowers and bushes. Nicole walked along the sidewalk until she reached a dirt path leading to the woods behind her neighborhood. Pebbles minimized the impact the rain from last night's storm had on the dirt path, but Nicole still had to evade a wet patch of sludge here or there.

An angry gray squirrel chattered at her from the top of a tree. Nicole scanned the ground for any sign of animal tracks larger than a dog, but it appeared largely undisturbed. She laughed at her foolishness.

Would a werewolf really favor the path over the underbrush?

Nicole supposed it depended where Ben had run .

Ben.

Nicole felt a pang of anguish. As she reached a fork in the path, Nicole remembered the last time she had gone for a walk in the woods—not during the day, but late at night. Less than a month ago, to watch a meteor shower. Maybe her parents attributed her transformation to a curse, but Nicole knew the truth.

Something had been with her in the woods that night.

Ben had been supposed to join her for a romantic moonlit picnic at the local nature trail, but he could not slip past his parents. Her own parents had gone to bed early that night, so Nicole packed a satchel with snacks, water, and a flannel blanket anyway. She turned on her phone's flashlight to navigate the trail.

A plump full moon sat low in the horizon. Nicole decided to turn off the flashlight setting on her phone before slipping it into her satchel. She allowed the moonlight to guide her through the woods to a clearing, then lay down on her blanket to stare up at the night sky in anticipation of the meteor shower. A few bats flittered across the moon. The air was warm, the breeze gentle and mild. She wished Ben was there to enjoy it with her.

Just as the first shooting star soared across the night sky, Nicole heard a low growl. She sat up, peering into the trees.

Hungry yellow eyes stared back at her.

Nicole rose to her feet, grabbing her satchel. She ran.

The beast ran after her.

Nicole did not look back until she reached the entrance of the trail, but something sharp swiped at her arm. A claw just barely nicked the skin of her bicep, enough to draw blood, but not enough to cause any serious damage.

The beast that had scratched her arm retreated with an angry howl when someone turned on their car's high beams. Her accidental savior was parked facing the entrance. Nicole shielded her eyes with her uninjured arm. The driver lowered their window to yell, "You shouldn't be here after dark. Didn't you see the sign?"

"Yeah, sorry. I just wanted to watch the meteor shower, and I figured there'd be less light pollution in the woods, but I'm going now," Nicole told them.

The speaker, a park ranger, insisted upon driving Nicole home. She concealed her wound, hugging her satchel to her chest. She'd never even considered the risk of rabies, let alone turning into a werewolf.

"I'm probably lucky it's lycanthropy and not rabies," Nicole mused to herself as she remembered that fateful night. "Unless I have both."

She whimpered.

Worse than her fear of rabies, Nicole worried Ben was gone for good. She wondered if she would still have gone to the woods that night had her parents shared their story sooner. Perhaps the old woman had not cursed them after all. Maybe she had seen their daughter's future and tried to warn them instead.

Nicole paused to sniff the air. She smelled something feral and strange, but it wasn't her attacker. Nicole didn't know how she knew, but she did. Whatever she smelled might be large, but it was wholly unique and not of this earth.

I've gotta get outta here, Nicole decided.

She ran back.

Now Nicole walked in the direction of her small town's main drag. Her nostrils flared at the scent of grilled hamburger. Following the scent, Nicole stepped into a small diner. Though her mother had made brunch after their talk, she still felt hungry.

Ravenous, in fact.

Nicole ordered lunch at the counter and sat down in a booth with her food.

"Mind if we join you?" a voice asked just as Nicole took a big bite of her cheeseburger. She looked up to see two of her friends from school. Bailey and Sofia sat down across from her in the booth. Bailey was tall and lanky with a straight blond ponytail, and Sofia was short and curvy, burgundy braids held back from her pretty face with a light blue sweatband. They both wore school shirts and track shorts.

Bailey took a big drink of her milkshake. "We took first place in cross country today." She grinned.

"Awesome."

Nicole picked at her fries. She hoped she sounded casual as she asked, "Where did you run? Just around town, or did you go through the woods?"

"The woods. If you don't wanna get dirty, you may as well stick to running track." Sofia stretched her legs out, showing Nicole traces of dried mud on her muscular calves. "I almost bit it, too, but Bailey kept me from falling down."

"Couldn't save Madeline, though. Slipped 'n fell right on her butt." Bailey laughed. "She still finished first out of all of us," she was quick to add.

Nicole forced a smile. "So…other than Maddie falling, did you guys see anything…uhm, interesting?" she asked.

"No…" Bailey exchanged a look with Sofia. "Hey, you feeling okay, Nicole? You seem a little out of it."

"Oh, duh." Sofia gave a rueful shake of her head. "She was up all night with Ben, weren't you, Nicole?"

Bailey grinned. "He's such a snack."

Nicole blanched.

"Oh, no. He didn't blow you off, did he?" Bailey asked.

"No," Nicole reassured her. "Just didn't feel good, so plans changed. That's all."

"Girl problems?" Sofia asked, with a look of sympathy.

"Something like that," Nicole replied.

"We just came in for celebratory milkshakes, but call me if you wanna hang out later," Bailey said.

The girls left. Nicole finished her burger. She almost felt guilty for the pleasure she took in devouring it, what with Ben missing and her entire life being turned upside down. If only she could have asked her friends for help. The three of them could cover more ground, but Nicole knew she had to handle this problem alone.

After she ate, Nicole walked back to the nature trail. This time, she picked the other direction when she reached the fork. The air cooled as clouds gathered to conceal the sun. Nicole smelled distant rain. She worried another storm would wash away any trace of Ben's path.

The wind changed direction. It carried the faint smell of…

Is that sandalwood?

Nicole followed her nose as she forced her way through the dense underbrush of the forest. She came upon a scrap of cloth snagged on a shrub. The color matched the green tee shirt Ben had worn the night before.

Nicole wondered how her sleuthing skills stacked up against Sherlock Holmes. *A werewolf detective. There should be such a show.*

She giggled, despite her growing apprehension.

Now her nose caught a whiff of something new: the metallic scent of blood.

Nicole looked around, but she saw nothing until the clouds moved. The sun reflected off an object a few yards away. She stumbled forward and reached down to pick up a shattered smartphone next to a rock. Whether the phone was off due to damage or a dead battery, she could not tell. She slipped it into her other back pocket, even though she knew it might implicate her as a suspect in Ben's disappearance.

She kept walking. Soon she heard the semi-regular thrum of traffic.

Nicole emerged in a clearing between the woods and a familiar road. She could only hope Ben had reached the road in time to find a ride home, but she no longer smelled even a hint of his cologne.

Nicole barely looked up when someone honked their horn at her. She tensed, hearing the vehicle make a U-turn. The driver of a red pickup truck with a rusty undercarriage pulled to a stop ahead of her. She noted a large shape, wild game of some sort, wrapped in a dark green tarp in the cargo bed of the truck. A couple of tall teenage boys in camouflage climbed down from either side of the pickup. They sauntered toward her.

"Hey Nikki, you seen Ben lately?" Harvey asked. He shared his cousin's dirty blond hair and green eyes but none of his looks or charm.

"Only Ben can call me that," Nicole reminded him.

Ignoring her, Harvey continued. "We caught a big ol' wolf when we were hunting last night. Wanted to show it to him."

"Thing's huge," contributed the other boy. Messy brown hair covered one of Jack's eyes. "We only have a deer permit, but it jumped right out at us." He tried to push his hair back with one hand, but it fell in his face again.

Nicole glanced at the tarp in the back of the pickup truck, raising an eyebrow. "You've been driving around town with a dead wolf in the back of your truck all day?" She wrinkled her nose in disgust.

"Only a couple hours," Harvey replied. "It was a night hunt, so we set up camp and slept until noon.

We just had lunch at the diner. Saw you walkin' down the street, so I thought we'd ask about Ben."

"Hey, you wanna see it?" Jack's eyes lit up with excitement. He walked back to the truck and started to raise the tarp.

"No, thanks." Nicole made another face as she shook her head.

"Aww, you sure?" Harvey looked disappointed.

"Positive."

"It's not all gory or anything, if that's what you're worried-"

"Hey dude, we got ourselves kind of a problem here," Jack interrupted. He lowered the end of the tarp, casting a furtive glance at the passing traffic.

"One sec." Harvey rolled his eyes. He walked back to Jack and peeked under the tarp.

His face drained of color as he looked back at Nicole. "We gotta go, Nikki."

"Later," said Jack. He exchanged a worried look with Harvey as they climbed back into the cab of their truck.

Nicole watched them go, frowning. For a horrible moment, she wondered if Ben's body was under the tarp.

"You dummy," she said aloud, rolling her eyes. "Even if I had attacked him, he wouldn't transform yet. Would he?"

Realizing she was arguing with herself, Nicole cast her own furtive glance up and down the street before she continued walking home.

Nicole returned to find her parents on the couch. Mrs. Farkas reclined against one side, her legs draped over the lap of Mr. Farkas. She looked up from her book at Nicole.

"You have a visitor in your room," she said with a smile.

"Make sure you keep the door open," Mr. Farkas added . "House rules."

That meant a boy.

Nicole hurried upstairs to her room.

Ben sat on her bed, his green eyes concerned as he looked up at her, a gift bag in his lap. "Hi Nikki, I...I brought you a present," he said, holding up the bag.

Nicole threw herself into his arms and squeezed hard.

Ben froze for a moment. Then he hugged Nicole back, burying his face in her tousled curls.

"I thought you were dead," she murmured into his shoulder, not mentioning that she might have been responsible for said death.

Ben patted her back. "No...I was just startled. I don't think I handled things as well as I could have," he said.

"Ben, I tried to eat you," Nicole said, pulling away to stare at him.

"That's just it," Ben said. "I don't think you did. After you changed, you sort of just sat back on your, uhm, haunches, and you, like, stared at me, wagging your tail. Then I flipped out and climbed out your window. I ran for the woods. You followed, but I think you saw a squirrel or something, and you got distracted. I'm a little embarrassed, to be honest."

"But I'm...I'm a werewolf," Nicole told him.

"Just on full moons, though, right?" Ben asked.

"It was my first time," Nicole said. "I...I think so. Something scratched me last month. When we were supposed to watch that meteor shower. You couldn't go, but I went anyway."

"You know, it's funny?" Ben looked away from Nicole to gaze out the window. "I always heard stories about monsters in the woods, but I never gave it any thought before now. I mean, not that you're a monster," he was quick to amend, his eyes returning to Nicole's face.

"I understand if you don't want to see me anymore." Nicole lowered her head. "I found your phone." She reached into her back pocket to return it to him.

Ben took it from her. "Nikki, of course I still want to see you. Just...maybe not, you know, then." He handed her the bag. "That's why I got you something...so you know I'm still thinking of you when we need to be apart."

Nicole sat down beside him. She opened the gift bag and began to sift through the tissues with trembling fingers.

"I dunno if it hurts, but I got some pain pills. And I know you love chocolate, so I got you some peanut butter cups and chocolate kisses. But the jerky seemed like a good idea, too," Ben explained.

Nicole blinked back her tears and grinned at him. "You really don't want to break up?"

"Eh, it's just lycanthropy. Couples deal with worse things." Ben frowned. "I am worried about one thing, though."

"What's that?" Nicole asked.

"There's still something in the woods," Ben said.

Nicole remembered her earlier encounter with his cousin. "I have a weird feeling we don't need to worry about that," she told him. "Call it instinct."

Ben raised an eyebrow but shrugged. Then he smiled at her.

Nicole threw herself back into his arms.

"That door had better still be open," Mr. Farkas hollered from downstairs.

Nicole pushed the door shut with her foot.

resting witch face

*T*oday is going to be a normal day.
    I'm going to be normal.
The brown eyes in the bathroom mirror appeared unconvinced. Samantha Landry sighed. She moisturized her skin and smoothed a small amount of argan oil onto the ends of her black straightened hair, which she pulled into a ponytail. The only makeup she applied was a tinted lip balm and mascara.

Samantha grabbed a well-worn heather gray sweatshirt out of the small closet to pull over her black tee shirt. Baggy jeans, scuffed sneakers, and large owlish sunglasses completed what Samantha thought wryly of as her uniform.

Samantha shouldered her bookbag as she left the small one-room apartment, miles from her parents' large suburban home a county away. She sometimes wondered if she would not be happier living at home with a longer commute but driving a car of her own instead of renting an apartment and relying on public transportation. She'd even considered staying in a dorm on campus. But she valued her independence. Maybe one day she would even take advantage of it.

For now, the extent of her social life consisted of working part-time in the campus bookstore and keeping up with a handful of former classmates online.

Samantha put on earbuds to listen to music, the volume set to low so she could remain alert to her surroundings. She walked down the street with her head lowered, stiffening as she approached the construction site where an old movie theater once stood. Before her arrival, the construction workers had harassed a young mother pushing her baby in a stroller.

Now the workers hounded a couple of preteen girls waiting for their school bus. The small brunette and lanky blonde wore khaki pants and hoodies over their polo shirts. Embarrassment inflamed their otherwise pale, freckled skin as they huddled close together, whispering in furtive voices.

The workers became silent as Samantha passed the site. The foreman shouted something unintelligible into his bullhorn. Everyone resumed working, except for one lone wolf who approached the fence, his narrow face eager. A couple workers nudged each other.

The lone wolf had short spiky black hair and the beginning of a five o-clock shadow. His denim overalls were too clean for this to be anything but his very first day of work. He held onto the chain links of the fence and leered at Samantha.

"Hey baby, what kinda curves you hidin' under all those clothes?"

Another worker tried to pull him away from the fence, but the lone wolf shrugged him off. The worker shook his head as he walked away. The foreman had already abandoned his bullhorn in favor of a smartphone, standing ready to dial.

"Hey bitch, I'm talkin' to you!"

Samantha winced. She tried to ignore the sudden whoosh made by a falling beam, and the crash and the crunch and the other wetter sounds as she hurried past the construction site.

The first accident happened when Samantha was thirteen. She was standing on the grassy median of a busy street, holding a sign to advertise a National Junior Honor Society car wash at a nearby gas station. An oversized tee shirt and loose shorts concealed her modest swimsuit and developing curves.

A man waiting at the light yelled something at Samantha that she did not understand but recognized as a sexual remark. She blushed. Another student told her to ignore him as he made an obscene gesture with his tongue and fingers. Then he drove his small car into a semi truck that was making a left turn.

Samantha had been terrified, but her parents attributed the accident to distracted driving, and assured her that she was not to blame for his carelessness. She did not believe them. And though she would never admit to something so awful, a small part of her felt vindicated.

The next accident occurred at a construction site, like the accident that happened today. That time Samantha felt more than vindicated; she felt powerful. She felt less powerful as time went on. Deep down, the accidents sickened her. So did the men, but Samantha would settle for their shame and remorse; she didn't want their blood.

"How do I make it stop?" a teenaged Samantha once wailed on the phone, feeling homesick for Louisiana and her grandmother's special gumbo.

"Not for you to stop," Mamere Landry had insisted. "Nothing wrong with you." Then she laughed when Samantha asked if her grandmother had put a gris-gris on anyone who bothered her. "People can put a gris-gris on themselves just fine. Don't need any help from me."

Samantha heard sirens in the distance, but she kept walking to the bus stop with her head down. There were plenty of other witnesses. The cops would not need to question everyone who happened to be walking by when the accident happened, and she did not want to miss the bus or her first class.

Once the bus arrived, Samantha faced the usual dilemma. She could sit beside someone else or take an empty seat and hope nobody objectionable joined her. Samantha decided to sit beside an elderly woman dressed in a cardigan and faded blue dress. The woman glanced up from her knitting to smile at her. She returned the smile with a shaky grin of her own.

Samantha adjusted her earbuds. Then she removed a sociology textbook from her book bag to review the last assigned chapter before class.

The woman shielded Samantha from unwelcome company for several stops before she gathered her knitting materials and exited the bus.

Samantha moved her book bag to the empty seat. She steeled herself when a middle-aged man in a rumpled business suit walked down the aisle toward her. She maintained a neutral expression as she felt his appraising eyes settle on her face.

"Pretty girl like you would be an absolute knockout, if only you smiled once in a while," the businessman advised Samantha as he walked by her seat. Then he tripped and hit his forehead on a metal pole, hard. The man pushed himself up and slid into a seat, groaning as he massaged his wounded temple.

Samantha smiled grimly at her reflection in the window. Her mirthless grin faded when she noticed few seats were left on the bus. Samantha moved her book bag to the floor.

A young man wearing a pink shirt and khaki pants boarded the bus at the next stop. He had smooth dark skin that offset his brilliant white teeth as he offered a friendly smile to the driver and other passengers. He sat beside Samantha without comment, holding his own book bag in his lap.

Samantha's cheeks grew warm when she noticed he smelled of citrus, sandalwood, and something spicier. The young man remained silent, his face and body relaxed.

The bus stopped outside the entrance of the college. Samantha removed her ear buds. She closed her textbook and slipped it into her book bag.

"I took that class last semester if you ever need somebody to study with," the man said as he stood up. The warmth in his voice sent a surprising jolt through Samantha. Though the sensation was not unpleasant, a sick feeling settled into the pit of her stomach.

The student walked off the bus. He greeted some other students and continued to walk to the student union. Samantha followed behind at a safe distance. After he strode ahead without incident, Samantha relaxed and turned to walk to her own class. She glanced back over her shoulder, but he had already disappeared in the swarm of other students.

"How's my boo?"

Samantha told her grandmother about the construction worker and the businessman. Then she told her about the college student. "It was so strange. He invited me to study, but nothing happened to him."

"What did he say?"

"He told me that he took the same class last year if I ever needed anyone to study with," Samantha replied. "Then he walked away."

"Sounds like a good boy to me. You do anything different?"

"No," Samantha replied. "Not a thing."

The next day Samantha wore a light blue shirt under her oversized sweatshirt and another pair of baggy jeans. She did not bother pulling her hair back into a ponytail.

To her relief, the city had shut down the construction site in order to hold an emergency inspection following yesterday's accident. Only men in suits and the foreman were present, examining the structure and various pieces of equipment. Samantha smiled at the middle school girls as she passed them to wait for her bus. The girls returned her smile, then resumed their animated conversation.

Once again, she chose the seat beside the elderly woman and took out a textbook.

The middle-aged businessman who had told Samantha to smile the day before boarded the bus a few stops later. She noticed a swollen purple goose egg of a bruise above his right eyebrow, a small butterfly bandage concealing a wound where his skin must have split. He avoided looking in her direction as he sat in an empty seat.

The college student boarded the bus at the next stop. Today he was wearing a bright blue shirt and white shorts. Samantha noticed his broad shoulders, strong legs, and the confident ease with which he carried himself. He smiled at her but sat across from the businessman.

Disappointed, Samantha continued to read, stealing occasional glances at the student. She felt silly, but she could not shake the compulsion. Samantha removed her ear buds as the bus pulled up to her stop.

"I hope you have a good day," the college student said with his velvety voice, flashing Samantha another engaging smile as he walked past her seat.

"You, too," she replied after a moment, but he

was already gone. Samantha scanned the crowd of students for a glimpse of him after she got off the bus without any luck. She shook her head at her foolishness and walked to class.

The next day was too warm for her sweatshirt, but Samantha felt strange wearing a fitted tee with baggy jeans. She searched through her dresser until she found a pair of jeans in her own size. She did not realize she had forgotten her music until she reached the construction site, so she ran back to her apartment to retrieve it.

Samantha returned in time to overhear the construction workers catcalling at a lone middle school student. The girl's blond hair had been pulled back in an elaborate braid, which inspired a few of the more suggestive remarks.

"Hey, sweet thang, where's your friend?"

"I just wanna grab a hold and-"

The construction worker made a lewd gesture to another worker. They both laughed.

The young girl blinked back tears. She scrunched her head down low in the collar of her polo shirt, as though willing herself to disappear. Samantha wondered if the girl wished her mother had spent less time lovingly styling her hair. She felt a pang of empathy.

Samantha strode over to the fence, holding her head high as she pushed up her sunglasses, treating the workers to the full weight of her intense stare. "Every day I see you bothering all the ladies walking by or waiting for the bus, no matter how young they are, but none of you have a thing to say to me," she said, surprised at the strength in her voice. Most of the workers looked away or lowered their heads, but the foreman stared at her agape. "Maybe you need to think of me the next time someone walks by, and you won't have anything to say to them, either."

Samantha lowered her sunglasses and remained standing between the workers and the girl until the school bus arrived.

Samantha missed her own bus by a few minutes. She would have to wait another twelve minutes for the next one. A couple teen boys in low baggy pants approached the bus stop and eyed Samantha, smirking.

"Don't even think about it," she told them.

They looked away and waited for the bus without comment.

Samantha did not recognize anyone when it arrived. She chose a seat by herself near the back. This bus was not as busy, so she read and listened to music uninterrupted on the way to school. Part of Samantha enjoyed the solitude; the other part felt sorry to have missed a certain someone's smile.

She didn't have to feel sorry for long.

After Samantha exited the bus, she saw the student standing with a group of classmates. He smiled at her and waved. Samantha lifted her hand in response, her lip curving up ever so slightly before she turned to walk to class.

The next day was sunny and warm. Samantha wore a long sleeveless sundress with a vibrant floral pattern in reds and greens and yellows. It grazed her ankles and felt silky against her skin. Perhaps sneakers looked silly with the dress, but Samantha didn't care. She tied a sweater around her waist. While the sun brought tantalizing warmth to her bare arms, she knew her classrooms would be much cooler.

Outside, a smiling mother pushed her stroller past the girls waiting for their school bus. She stopped for them to coo over her baby and talk about their excitement for warmer days to come. The construction site buzzed with activity, but nobody made any catcalls. Samantha grinned at the foreman. His lips twitched.

"That's a lovely scarf," Samantha told the elderly woman as she sat down beside her on the bus. "I can't wait to see what you make next."

"Thank you." A smile brightened the woman's weathered face. "I don't think I've seen you wear a dress before. It's very pretty."

Samantha started to remove her music and text-book from her book bag but changed her mind and left the music in the pouch. After the old woman exited the bus a few stops later, the middle-aged businessman entered the bus on the next stop. His bruise was no longer swollen, the purple fading to green and yellow. Samantha moved over to make room, amusement crinkling the corner of her eyes. He noted the lack of seats and sat beside her.

Samantha continued reading, but she glanced up when the student boarded the bus next, wearing an emerald green shirt and denim shorts. He grinned, grabbing hold of a bar near her seat, and Samantha smiled softly in return. This time he waited for Samantha outside the bus, standing next to a campus map with his hands in his pockets and a rueful grin on his face.

"Hi. I'm Jaden."

"Sam." She pushed back her sunglasses.

Jaden walked with Samantha to her class, then asked her to meet him at the student union for lunch later that day. They discussed everything from sociology to their favorite music over deli sandwiches and coffee, and they sat beside each other on the bus to go home.

"You want to hang out again tomorrow?"

"I'll save you a seat." Samantha grinned.

"Callin' again so soon, honeychile?" Mamere Landry asked, a note of concern entering her voice. "What happened now?"

"Nothing." Samantha paused. "And everything."

She explained how the construction workers had stopped bothering people, and how nobody gave Samantha a hard time on the bus. Then she told her grandmother about Jaden.

"Told you he was a good boy," Mamere Landry boasted. "You do anything different?"

Everything, Samantha started to say, and in a way, it was the truth, but that was not her grandmother's point, was it?

"Not a thing," Samantha finally answered, smiling.

the game

Vincent Ricci walked down the stairs and through the double doors into a dimly lit venue known as The Cellar. The Cellar was not really a cellar; it was the name of an underground café on campus. The café had ample seating, a coffee kiosk, and a stage utilized for everything from poetry slams to karaoke on theme nights.

Vincent scanned the crowd.

Nothing happened on Mondays. Vincent had vowed to avoid poetry slams *and* karaoke for a while. Tabletop Tuesdays were out by virtue of being Tabletop Tuesdays. No need to delve into *that* crowd. He needed to lay low for a while, but he hadn't yet exhausted his supply of moody poetesses and wannabe pop stars.

Monday, though...

Monday had potential.

It was just a normal theme-free night. That meant regulars were unlikely. Any number of prospects might stop by the Cellar to study or view their social media accounts away from the prying eyes of nosy roommates.

Vincent ran a hand through his dark hair as he approached the coffee kiosk. He noticed another missing person poster on the community board affixed to a wall behind the counter, the fifth poster in less than a year. A pretty coed smiled back at him from a colored photo.

What a shame.

She looked like fun.

Another poster showed the photo of a young man Vincent vaguely recognized from one of his classes last semester, but he did not have time to consider it before a pretty barista with brown hair pulled back in a sleek ponytail and hazel eyes turned to regard him with a sour expression. Her voice dripped with disdain as she asked, "Your usual, Vinny?"

Natalie.

Damn.

Vincent forgot Natalie worked on Mondays.

He offered her his most dazzling smile, but Natalie turned her back and began making his mocha latte. Vincent could only hope she wouldn't spit in it. When Natalie turned around, the smirk on her face alarmed him.

Vincent looked at his latte, understanding the real reason behind Natalie's smirk. The foam art consisted of a sad looking pig under the word "you."

He smiled, handing Natalie his money. She tried to avoid physical contact, but Vincent brushed his fingertips against the palm of her hand.

"Why are you like this?" Natalie kept her head

down as she made change.

He laughed. "Because I can be."

Vincent flashed another wide grin as Natalie handed him his change. He maintained eye contact as he slipped a dollar bill into the front pocket of her apron. Natalie took out the dollar and shoved it into her back pocket before she tore off the apron. She gave Vincent one last withering glare before storming into the stock room to clock out.

Vincent turned and leaned against the counter to take a sip of his mocha latte. He noticed a diminutive woman sitting by herself in a booth at the far end of the Cellar. She had dark brows and lashes, but her long blond hair shone like strands of gold and silver beneath the light of the Tiffany lamp.

Vincent strolled over to the booth. The blonde did not look up from her book.

He slid into the seat across from her. "My mom read that to me when I was a kid," Vincent told her.

"I read it myself when I was a kid." She turned to the next page. "This time I'm reading it for a class on Victorian literature."

"I won't bother you then." Vincent started to rise.

"You're not bothering me. I'm just waiting for you to give me a reason to put my book down."

Feisty.

He sat down, plucked the book from her hands, closed it, and set it on the table. Vincent leaned back with a satisfied smirk.

"An 'A' for effort." She gazed at him with the barest hint of a smile. "But that wasn't the assignment."

"So, you're playing teacher now." Vincent's grin widened.

"I don't like games," she admitted. "I'm Selena."

"Vinny."

"So, Vinny, what do you like to do for fun?" Selena tucked a strand of shimmering blond hair behind her ear. "I doubt you spend all of your time waiting in dark places for someone to catch your attention."

"Not all my time, no." Vincent laughed.

"Do you like to hike?" Selena slid out of the booth to join Vincent on his side. He felt a jolt of anticipation from the warmth of her leg pressing against his own. "I know this amazing trail beyond Lookout Point. It leads to a clearing that's the perfect spot for stargazing."

"Lookout Point, huh?"

Vincent ran his fingers through his hair. He hoped that Selena did not pick up on his nervousness. He had been hearing some wild stories about the local make-out spot lately.

Strange noises.

Scary monsters.

Typical urban legend stuff, but the stories gave him pause.

Could they have anything to do with all the missing coeds?

"You're not scared, are you?" Selena's dark blue...no, *violet* eyes - a trick of the light, no doubt - searched his as she squeezed his leg above his knee.

"Hardly." Taken aback by her forwardness, Vincent grabbed her hand. He nudged her out of the booth. "We can take my car. I happen to know a shortcut."

"Are you sure you wouldn't prefer to stay in the car where it's warm and cozy?" Vincent took a quick look at Selena as he backed his black coupe into a parking spot. Lookout Point was otherwise deserted.

"We're a bit old for parking." Selena smiled. She grabbed her hoodie from the seat as she exited the car. Selena slipped it on over her tank top and zipped it halfway. Vincent felt a twinge of disappointment.

"So, where's this trail of yours?" Vincent cast a sidelong glance at her legs as he exited the coupe.

Selena raised a slender but muscular arm to indicate a dirt path that was framed on either side by trees and lush fauna. Though a big waxing moon brightened the sky, darkness enveloped the pair as they entered the woods. Vincent jumped at a rustling sound near his feet.

"Garter snake," Selena assured him, chuckling. She grabbed his hand. Vincent allowed her to guide him deeper into the forest. Soon he heard the sound of running water cascading over rocks and pebbles. "The creek leads to a pond off the path a little way. Want to see if it's deep enough for a swim?"

"I didn't bring my suit."

"Neither did I." Selena winked at Vincent. She darted off through the dense underbrush, deftly avoiding shrubs and fallen logs.

Vincent followed her. Something buzzed near his ear. When he swatted at his neck, his hand came away red with his own blood... and the blood of whatever else the mosquito had been feeding on.

Vincent found himself wondering if pursuing Selena was more trouble than she was worth. Then he thought of her shapely legs and the curve of her breasts under her tank top. Vincent pushed deeper into the woods. The underbrush scraped his legs, piercing his skin through his jeans. He moved one tree branch out of his way, only to get scratched in the forehead by another higher branch he had not seen. A thin trail of blood trickled down his forehead from the shallow cut, attracting more mosquitoes.

By the time Vincent arrived at the pond, his enthusiasm had given way to annoyance. Then he saw Selena smiling up at him from the moonlit water. Her clothes sat in a tidy pile on a nearby tree stump. The ripples she created in the pond while treading water distorted his view of her naked body.

Vincent struggled to shed his own shoes and clothing.

Then he jumped into the pond.

It was deeper than Vincent expected and very cold. He felt a stab of panic, unsure of which way was up and which was down. Using the reflection of the moon to reorient himself, Vincent swam up. When he reached the surface, he took several deep, gasping breaths of air. Vincent did not see Selena anywhere.

"Selena?"

No answer.

"Selena!"

Somewhere in the distance, the deep bass of an ancient horn boomed, and the forest trembled. Vincent splashed to shore, but he found no sign of Selena or his clothing.

"That bitch!"

His thin boxer briefs clung to his shivering body after he pushed himself out of the pond. Vincent tried to backtrack in hopes of finding the main path. He yelped each time a pine needle punctured his feet.

Angry barks and howls pierced the silence of the woods. As their snarls grew closer, Vincent changed direction. "What in the hell is going on?" he wondered aloud.

Vincent squealed as something furry brushed against his leg. The moonlight revealed a small, reddish animal running away. Remembering the sound of the strange horn, he wondered if fox hunting was a thing around here.

Vincent had grown up in the city. He knew very little about life in a small rural town, but he felt certain he did not want a bunch of trigger-happy hicks in camouflage finding him alone in the woods wearing only his underwear. And he definitely did not want their hound dogs to tear him apart.

Vincent yelped and winced in pain as his bare feet continued to find every sharp rock and thorny plant in his path with devastating accuracy. Ravenous mosquitoes feasted on him despite his efforts to slap them away.

When Vincent tripped over a fallen tree branch, he scraped his knees and sliced the palm of his hand open on a rock. Even without looking, he sensed this cut was deep. His fingers tingled, growing numb.

Something awful occurred to Vincent as he rolled onto his back and clutched his bleeding hand to his chest. Nobody had any idea where he was, and he did not know if anyone would even notice or care if he went missing.

Vincent rarely encountered his roommate.

He only called his parents every other week.

His friends - acquaintances, really - might wonder where he was by the time Friday night rolled around, but no sooner than that.

Vincent never felt so alone.

Maybe his face would someday be found among the other missing-people posters around campus. Perhaps Natalie would stick it on a dart board. While the list of people who would miss Vincent was short, the list of women with a grudge was longer.

A triumphant howl interrupted Vincent's misery. A muscular black dog the size of a bear crashed through the underbrush. It landed with its massive paws on his chest. The sharp claws sliced into his exposed flesh. A drop of saliva splashed on his cheek, burning like acid. The dog looked like some sort of terrible hell beast with its glowing red eyes. Jagged bloodstained teeth lined its powerful jaws.

Vincent closed his eyes and turned his head. He trembled in anticipation of the searing pain that would come when the hellhound ripped his throat apart.

Instead, it sat back on its haunches. Its mistress had called it off.

Selena pushed back the hood of her dark cloak to smile down at Vincent. Her silver and gold hair shimmered in the moonlight, and her violet eyes – not a trick of the light, after all - sparkled with amusement. Only now did Vincent notice her long, pointed ears. A strap of leather secured a bow and quiver to her back. The pale silky shift she wore under her cloak revealed a leather garter holding a sharp knife at her thigh .

"Oh, Vinny," Selena purred into his ear as she knelt down before him to stroke his cheek. "You're not having a very good night, are you?"

She ran her fingers through his hair. He shivered at her touch. Selena tightened her grip and yanked his head back to expose his neck. The hellhound's breath was hot against his throat once more.

"What are you?" Vincent asked. "Why are you like this?"

"I am beyond your capacity to comprehend, and this is a far more noteworthy end than your kind deserves."

The hellhound started to growl again, deep in its throat, as another beast lumbered into the clearing. Vincent squinted at a large hulking shape with curved horns on either side of its wolfish head.

"Not you again," Selena said, turning toward the new beast. She released her grip on Vincent's hair as she rose, hands on her hips in annoyance. "Tonight is my night. These woods are mine until dawn."

The beast roared in reply as it raced toward the hellhound. The two collided in a fearsome tornado of claws and saliva and gnashing fangs.

Vincent rolled over, pushed himself up. He began to run. An arrow flew past his head, so close he felt the wind blowing off it, and lodged itself into a tree to his right. More arrows showered the ground around his feet as he ran.

Vincent saw a glimmer of light penetrating the trees ahead. He tore through the thorny, tangled underbrush as another arrow nicked his shoulder.

He screamed in pain and fell forward onto asphalt. The headlights of a car shone on his pale skin.

"Bad date?" a female voice demurred as someone exited the driver's side of the car. Slender fingers appeared in front of Vincent's face. He grudgingly accepted the hand with his unscathed one as he rose to his feet.

"Who the hell is this clown?" a male voice demanded.

Vincent looked up at a tall muscular man with brown hair, brown eyes, and broad shoulders. The man wore jeans and a college letterman jacket, which meant he was at least a sophomore. Vincent recognized him as a running back on the football team.

Natalie had traded up.

Right now, she gazed at Vincent with a look of amusement and pity in the place of her usual anger and resentment.

"He's my...he's, uhm..." Natalie trailed off. "He's just some idiot from school. We should give him a lift back to campus."

"We're cutting our night short for him?" the new boyfriend started to complain.

Vincent protested, "But I'm parked right over there."

He pointed, but his car was gone. Vincent's hand dropped to his side as he gaped at nothing. The three heard a howl of rage beyond the tree line.

"Then again, we can just Netflix and chill instead after we drop his ass off at the dorms or wherever he stays." The running back gave Vincent the side eye before he climbed into the front passenger seat of Natalie's car.

Vincent allowed Natalie to help him into the back seat. She wrapped a thin fleece blanket over his shoulders before pulling some wipes from a bag in the center console to clean the blood from his chest. Then she turned over his hand.

"Oh, Vinny, what on earth have you done to yourself?"

Her voice sounded more tender than he ever heard it before. Her touch was just as gentle as she cleaned his palm. "I don't think I have any bandages that are big enough. Hold the wipe against it for now. You should really get this looked at by campus health in the morning."

He met her eyes, but only for a moment. They both jumped at the sound of another howl.

Closer now.

"Hey Nat, you done playin' nurse?"

Natalie gave Vincent another pitying look before climbing up into the front seat of the car to drive. He sat in quiet contemplation as they left Selena and her hellhound behind, his injured hand throbbing in pain.

Tomorrow would be Tabletop Tuesday at the Cellar.

Vincent wondered if he should check it out or stay in his room to play solitaire until the inevitable rumors about his crawl of shame died down. He tried to remember if Natalie worked on Tuesdays. He considered asking but changed his mind after he saw the running back resting his hand on her thigh.

Natalie glanced at him in the rearview mirror on the drive back to campus every now and then, but he avoided her eyes.

Solitaire it would be.

queen bee

"**B**ad boys are boring."

Allison Carter raised an eyebrow. "What?"

"Bad boys are boring," Taylor White repeated. She inclined her head in the direction of the lockers across the hall, where Brandon Fuller, a dark-haired senior in a letterman's jacket, leaned over a cheerleader. He whispered something in her ear. She giggled.

"Didn't you go out once?" Allison asked.

"Yes, and he was boring." Taylor pulled her long blond hair into a ponytail. "Why do you think it was just the once?"

"Well, 'one and done' fits the whole 'bad boy' persona," Allison noted. "What was boring about him?"

"Too fast and no...uhm...hmm." Taylor paused as she searched for the right word. "Skill sounds too clinical, and it's not like he was completely hopeless. Finesse," she decided. "And all of the same stupid lines as every other guy I've dated. I bet he's using them on her right now." Taylor glanced across the hall as she slipped a smartphone out of her back pocket. "Such a waste of a nice ass, too."

Allison watched with mild curiosity as Taylor scrolled through pictures of people, some Allison recognized, on one of her social media accounts. "Why not date someone other than a bad boy for a change?"

Taylor sighed. "It's always same shit, different... well, you know." She grinned, wiggling her index finger.

Allison blushed.

"I'm just so over high school." With another heavy sigh, Taylor turned to lean back against her locker. "And it's not just the guys."

"Since when do you date girls?" Allison's blush deepened as the words left her mouth.

"Possibly in the not-so-distant future, but that's not what I mean." Taylor laughed. "Like, check this out." She displayed a smiling photo of three senior girls holding plastic cups. "Abigail and Haylie totally abandoned Jessica after she got wasted on Saturday, and I had to take her drunk ass home before somebody took advantage of her."

"I didn't know there was a party," Allison said.

"Oh. Sorry. Jeffrey made a public post inviting everyone. I forgot you're totally offline," Taylor said. "You didn't miss much, I swear. It was lame."

"Sounds like it," Allison agreed, though her tone betrayed her wistfulness. She did not have a smartphone. Her mother even limited her internet access on the computer at home to doing research for school--no social media allowed.

"I swear I see the same tired dramas play out

over and over again, and everyone keeps coming back for the show." Taylor resumed her ranting as she stared across the hall. "Like Lauren over there, totally buying Brandon's act. Doesn't she know he's already been through half the squad?"

Allison chewed the inside of her lower lip, watching Brandon and Lauren across the hall. She wondered if he was as bad as Taylor said. A sudden image of Brandon leaning down to kiss Allison appeared in her mind's eye. She shivered (with revulsion, she decided) as she tried to scrub the unwelcome image from her brain.

"Ugh!"

Brandon and the cheerleader stopped talking to stare in her direction. Allison tried to play off her reaction like she was still looking at something on Taylor's phone. "You're right," she whispered. "What is wrong with us?"

Taylor arched a perfectly sculpted eyebrow.

"People, I mean."

"Dunno." Taylor shrugged. "But it's probably the reason aliens haven't reached out to us. Any advanced society would not have the patience for our stupidity."

"Allie Carter, please come to the Guidance office."

Allison groaned as the announcement repeated. The rest of her homeroom class watched her leave. Brandon leaned back in his chair and gave her the usual once-over, his eyes lingering on her chest.

Had she really started to fantasize about him earlier?

Yuck.

Allison wrinkled her nose.

She wondered what her guidance counselor wanted. The local college had already sent an acceptance letter and information about the dorms. Apart from her friendship with Taylor, Allison kept to herself and stayed out of trouble.

When Allison arrived in the counselor's office, she found a girl standing there, wearing a low-cut sweater that accentuated her curves and a pair of fashionably distressed designer jeans. She had a luxurious mane of chestnut hair, green eyes, and a big smile. Allison stared at her in confusion instead of returning her grin.

The guidance counselor introduced the new girl as Melissa Beckett. "I thought you could show Melissa around the school. You have some AP courses together, so I assigned her to your homeroom," Miss Johnson said in her cloying, chipper tone as she handed Allison a copy of Melissa's schedule.

Allison offered Melissa a tentative smile, feeling self-conscious in her baggy sweater and rumpled jeans . She looked down at the schedule. Allison found it hard to believe that someone as beautiful and well-dressed as Melissa bothered with AP homework when she could be out on a date instead.

"Uhm, so I guess I should show you where your other classes are first, and then we can finish the tour at our home room. Sound good, Melissa?"

"Please, call me Mel."

When Allison heard the name Mel, she thought of the large, grumpy but lovable cook at her favorite local diner, not a tall, curvy brunette who rivaled even Taylor in beauty, but she kept the observation to herself. "Most people call me Allie."

In truth, most people did not call her anything or speak to her much at all, but that was fine with Allison. She led Melissa out of the office. Allison saw a dozen male heads turn at once when they passed the gym, and a sophomore nearly walked into a wall.

Melissa appeared oblivious. "This seems like a really nice school."

"It's alright, I guess." Allison shrugged. "I grew up here. It's all I've ever known."

"I envy you." Melissa frowned. "I never seem to stay in any place for long."

"Military brat?"

Melissa stared at her. Allison bit her lip, worried she had offended the new girl.

"Something like that."

Melissa's smile returned, but it did not quite reach her eyes. The two continued to walk down the hall in what Allison hoped was a companionable rather than awkward silence. She considered telling Melissa that her father had walked out on her mom before she was born, but decided it was too soon to reveal such personal details about her life.

Melissa paused, appraising Allison's profile. When Allison turned to look at her with a quizzical tilt to her head, Melissa tugged on one of her braided pigtails. "Have you ever considered wearing your hair down?" She let go of the pigtail to tuck a loose strand of mousy brown hair behind Allison's ear.

Allison blinked, taken aback by the intimate gesture. "I do wear it down sometimes." She walked a few more steps before stopping. "Uhm, here's our home room."

Allison opened the door and followed Melissa inside. Brandon stared unabashedly at the new girl, his eyes lingering over pretty much everything. Allison could not decide if she felt relieved or disappointed to be spared another one of his leers in her direction.

"This seat's available." Brandon gestured to the seat beside his with a broad grin.

"I think I'd rather sit closer to the window, but thank you." Melissa walked to a different empty seat on the other side of the classroom.

Allison bit her lower lip to stifle a smile as she took her own seat behind Melissa.

The rest of the morning was uneventful, at least for Allison. Melissa dazzled classmates and teachers alike with her wit and insights in AP English and AP History. Allison felt a small twinge of relief to have a Melissa-free clarinet lesson fourth period before lunch.

"This is..." Allison started to say.

"Mel," Taylor finished, grinning. She sat down at the lunch table across from Allison and beside Melissa, her face flushed. "We have gym together. It was amazing. You should've seen Emma's face when we beat her in doubles tennis."

"Hope Emma wasn't too disappointed about losing the match. She plays very well," Melissa observed.

Allison raised an eyebrow. "Since when do you

care about tennis?" she asked Taylor.

"I like winning."

For a moment, Taylor's blue eyes appeared to glow with a strange green fire.

Allison inhaled sharply. Melissa smiled and winked.

Allison felt her blood run cold.

Allison had AP Calculus and AP Physics with Melissa after lunch, but she did not see Taylor again until study hall last period. It was her only class with Taylor, but Melissa had it, too. The two girls were already deep in conversation when Allison entered the room. She chose a seat in front.

Brandon sauntered into the room from a different class a few moments after the bell rang.

He didn't appear to be holding a hall pass. "I gotta talk to someone real quick."

The teacher rolled her eyes, but she did not make him return to his own room. He walked straight back to Taylor and Melissa. Allison pretended to be immersed in her math assignment, but inclined her head to listen.

"You're new, so I guess I can give you a pass on not knowing who I am," he said. "I might even take you to dinner some time, if you feel like making it up to me."

"I know who you are." Melissa said. "I don't mess with boys my friends have dated."

Taylor's jaw dropped. "But I never said..."

Now Allison was openly staring, but so were her classmates.

Even the teacher looked ready to intervene.

Brandon looked at Taylor as if he had only just noticed her. "Oh, hey, Taylor. You never called me back. Thought maybe you decided you didn't like me."

"I texted you several times." Taylor glared at him. "And I don't. Like you, I mean."

Brandon opened his mouth to speak, but hesitated. He raised his hands, looking uncharacteristically abashed. Allison might have found it endearing if she did not know him better.

"You can leave now," Melissa told him.

Brandon looked back and forth between Melissa and Taylor. He turned and saw everyone watching. His expression hardened when his gaze settled on Allison's face. "What are you lookin' at?"

Allison felt her cheeks and ears grow warm. She looked down at her assignment, ignoring him as he strode by her table and out of the room.

The next morning, Allison groaned inwardly when she saw Taylor and Melissa standing beside her locker.

"Oh, hi, Allie." Taylor smiled.

"We were just talking about you," Melissa added.

Allison did not like the sound of that. She forced herself to return their smiles, but feared hers resembled a grimace instead. Even her 'hello' sounded strained to her ears.

"I thought you were gonna wear your hair down today." Melissa frowned, appearing disappointed.

Self-conscious, Allison reached up to touch her hair, which had been pulled back into a single braid.

"No, I mean we talked about it, but I never said I…"

She trailed off as Brandon walked up to them. Her ears burned as she remembered him snapping at her yesterday.

Brandon appeared almost contrite as he stopped in front of Taylor, his hands tucked into the pockets of his letterman's jacket. "So, I've been trying to figure out what your problem is, and I finally remember what happened. I dropped my phone into the toilet, so I had to replace it. That's why I never got any of your texts. Guess I should've tried talking to you, but I took for granted you blew me off after our, uhm, you know, that night. That was dumb."

"Yeah, it was," Taylor agreed. She turned away from Brandon to look at Allison. "Mel's right, you know. You really should wear your hair down. You'd look so pretty." Taylor smoothed Allison's hair back from her face.

Allison's cheeks warmed at Taylor's touch.

Brandon sighed. Melissa and Taylor rolled their eyes at each other but otherwise ignored him. Agitated, he ran a hand through his hair as he stalked off to homeroom. Once he was out of sight, Taylor laughed. "What's his deal?"

"You should tell someone he's bothering you," Allison said.

"I kinda like the attention," Taylor admitted.

"You don't, do you?" Melissa asked Allison, who tilted her head in confusion. "Like the attention, I mean," she clarified as she peered into Allison's face.

Allison tried not to squirm under the new girl's searching gaze. "No, I mean, yes. I dunno. I'm not sure what I'd do with someone's attention if I got any."

Allison only seemed to attract negative attention, so she tried hard to stay off everyone's radar. Still, she felt lonely sometimes. Though she spent a lot of time with Taylor at school, she doubted Taylor would say they were besties. Now that Melissa was in the picture, she worried she would lose what little friendship they had.

"You know, it doesn't have to be that way."

Allison stared at Melissa.

Was she responding to her words or her thoughts?

"I bet you could have anybody you wanted if you put yourself out there."

"I really just want to survive high school in one piece." Allison shrugged.

The bell rang. Melissa didn't say anything as they walked to their homeroom, but Allison noticed the way she looked at her. Contemplative, like she was trying to work something out.

Melissa did not appear to notice when Brandon grabbed Allison by the elbow and pulled her around the corner after homeroom. He pressed his free hand against the wall, pinning her. Allison was too surprised to jerk her arm away from Brandon or say anything. Instead she stared at him, her eyes wide.

"You gotta talk to Taylor for me." Brandon's brown eyes bore into hers as his grip on her arm tightened. The smell of his aftershave burned her nose.

"You're hurting me." Allison struggled to pull

her arm free of his grasp.

Brandon looked startled. He glanced down at his hand. His fingers were leaving visible indentations on Allison's arm. "I'm sorry." He released her elbow, but placed his hand on her shoulder. "I didn't mean to hurt you, or Taylor. I just can't stop thinking about her, and she won't talk to me when Melissa's around."

"I don't think Taylor wants to talk to you," Allison said. "Why can't you just let it go?"

Brandon shrugged. "I get off on a challenge."

For a moment, his dark eyes glowed with the same green fire Allison had seen in Taylor's eyes yesterday. She pulled away from Brandon and ducked under his other arm to escape, then ran to her next class.

Allison avoided Melissa for the rest of the morning. During lunch, she decided to take her food outside to eat on a grassy hill beside a tree.

She pushed up the sleeve of her hoodie to see faint bruises above her elbow where Brandon had grabbed her. Upon closer inspection, she even noticed red half-moons from his nails. She pulled the sleeve down and put away her half-eaten sandwich. Unease gnawed at her stomach.

In AP Calculus, a starry-eyed Joey Mason handed Melissa a piece of lined paper. It appeared to be last night's assignment.

Allison pulled him aside after class, softening her grip when she remembered the way Brandon had grabbed her earlier. "Have you been doing Melissa's homework for her?"

The small boy ran a hand through his brown disheveled hair. "I love helping." Joey's lips curled into a rueful smile. "Melissa says I'm her best helper."

If Joey had a tail, it would be wagging.

Allison did not even flinch when his brown eyes glowed with an all too familiar green fire.

"Are you okay?" Melissa asked as she sat down next to Allison in AP Physics. "You've been very distant today."

"I didn't think you'd notice," Allison said. "You're always surrounded by people wanting to talk to you."

"You don't have to be jealous," Melissa told her.

"I...I'm not jealous," Allison muttered, sinking lower in her seat. She avoided Melissa's eyes for the rest of class. Let her think she was jealous; it felt safer than the alternative.

Once again, Allison selected a seat in front of the room during study hall. Melissa and Taylor sat in the back with their heads close together, whispering to one another. Allison felt certain they were looking at her, but she ignored them and worked on the rough draft of an essay for AP English.

"Taylor, wait!"

Brandon stood outside the classroom after study hall ended that afternoon.

"I don't have anything to say to you," Taylor told Brandon. She brushed past him to follow Melissa to the stairs.

"Just hear me out."

Brandon grabbed Taylor's wrist.

"Let go of me!"

Taylor pulled her wrist free as she pivoted away from him. Brandon lost his footing. His eyes widened with surprise as he sailed past the girls down the stairs.

Allison heard a sickening thud when his head hit the floor. She looked from his prone body to Taylor and Melissa. Allison thought she saw the trace of a cruel smile on Melissa's pretty face.

Melissa turned to stare at Taylor, her eyes wide. "What did you do?"

"I didn't mean to," Taylor whispered, backing away. Students looked between Brandon's prone form at the base of the stairs and Taylor, their expressions ranging from accusing to frightened.

Melissa's green eyes met Allison's gaze. She did not break eye contact until a teacher approached Brandon, talking into a smartphone.

"It was an accident," Melissa told him as she ran down the stairs. "She never meant for him to fall," Melissa added. She looked up the stairs at Taylor, her lips curling into another brief but unmistakable smirk.

Taylor leaned against a wall and slid down until she sat in a despondent slump, staring at the opposite wall, her eyes wide but unseeing. Allison knelt down to comfort her friend. She put a hand on the girl's shoulder, but Taylor jerked free. Allison rose, frowning. She followed the rest of the students to another stairwell.

"It's not like he died or anything. They don't

even know if the paralysis is permanent," Allison overheard Melissa tell Taylor by the lockers the next day.

Taylor moaned.

"Don't feel bad. I'm sure nobody blames you." Melissa put a hand on Taylor's shoulder.

Taylor's eyes were bloodshot; her hair hung in tangles. She shrugged off Melissa's hand, darting away down the hall. Other students whispered to each other as she passed.

Melissa noticed Allison. Her cruel green eyes narrowed as she tilted her head. Allison sensed something almost predatory about the sudden movement, like a super-smart raptor in one of those dinosaur movies, calculating its next move. She looked away, her skin crawling.

Allison kept her distance the rest of the day, but observed another exchange of work between Joey and Melissa in the afternoon. Taylor did not come to study hall.

Taylor did not come to school the following morning either. Allison spent another quiet lunch outside. Maybe she could share her new favorite spot with Taylor now that the love affair with Melissa appeared to be over. If Taylor ever came back. Allison missed Taylor's sharp humor and keen insights.

Joey occupied Melissa's attention in the afternoon. Allison could sense the girl's annoyance as he chattered at her in the hallway on the way to AP Calculus.

Melissa came to an abrupt stop near a stairwell that led to the basement. Allison tried not to stare as the girl placed a hand on Joey's forearm. Melissa leaned down to whisper something in his ear. Joey's cheeks flamed, but he nodded at her.

Melissa began to walk down the stairs.

Joey followed.

Allison narrowed her eyes. Nobody else seemed to notice her as she took several slow, deliberate steps after them.

Allison stopped just before the stairwell. She leaned against the wall, straining to listen.

The bell rang to signal the start of next period.

Now that the hall was quiet, Allison could hear murmuring in the basement; then, a moan. She made a face. The moan gave way to muffled screams, followed by silence.

No.

Not silence.

Wet, slippery sounds and the occasional crunch.

Allison's eyes widened. She ran to the nurse's office for a late pass. At least she did not have to lie about feeling sick to her stomach. Allison did not know what to do next, but she knew she needed to stay off the school's radar as much as Melissa's.

The only available seat when Allison arrived at AP Calculus was behind Melissa. "You feeling okay, Allie?" The new girl turned around with a look of faux concern that did not quite reach her eyes.

"Girl problems," Allison whispered. She placed a hand on her lower belly, giving Melissa her most pitiful look as she slid down in her chair.

Melissa raised an eyebrow but didn't press the issue.

Allison focused on taking notes for the duration of class. When the bell rang, she rose to gather her belongings. Melissa reached for her hand.

"Sorry, gotta go."

Allison flashed Melissa a grin she could only hope did not look as forced as it felt. Under normal circumstances, Melissa might shrug it off as Allison's usual awkward manner or discomfort from her period, but these were not normal circumstances. Allison hurried away, afraid to look back.

The weekend could not come soon enough, Allison decided as she walked into her homeroom the next morning. She made a point of arriving just before the bell so Melissa would not have time to talk to her, but she had no reason to worry. Melissa was swarmed by a gaggle of girls. She did not even look up when Allison walked in.

That morning Allison realized Joey was not Melissa's only AP homework supplier. Boys and girls alike seemed happy to do her bidding. Allison shuddered to think what Melissa promised them in return for their work. One of those suppliers stopped Allison in the hallway before lunch.

"You eating outside, Allie?" Riley Lawrence asked, her face eager. "Because Mel's waiting for you in your favorite spot. She really needs to talk to you."

Allison raised her eyebrows. "I'm not feeling so hot. I'm gonna lay down in the nurse's office instead." Allison pressed both hands against her lower belly. Even a pretend period could last more than a day if she needed it to.

Allison saw no sign of Melissa when she arrived at their AP Calculus class. She did not have time to consider the reason for Melissa's absence, because Mrs. Harrison beckoned to her before class started.

"Miss Johnson needs to see you in guidance."

Allison groaned inwardly. She needed to pass the stairwell Melissa had led Joey down yesterday on her way to the guidance office.

When the bell rang, the hall emptied.

Allison quickened her pace.

Something whipped out of the stairwell and wrapped itself around her ankle, starting to pull her off balance. Allison gasped. Another strange appendage, slimy yet powerful, wrapped around her mouth before she could scream. She blacked out when her head banged against one of the stairs on the way down.

Allison opened her eyes and sat up. Her head throbbed.

She looked around the basement for any signs of her captor-- or Joey's remains. But all Allison observed was a darker patch of cement on the floor near a furnace. She shuddered.

"I know it's not the coziest environment, but I just wanted to find someplace we could talk in private." Melissa walked up behind her.

Allison knew what Melissa was, or at least what she wasn't, and she knew Melissa knew it. Although she wanted to scream for help, Allison doubted anyone would hear. She decided to push down her fear and cut to the chase instead. She stood up to face Melissa.

"Are you eating people? You're eating people, aren't you?"

"No!" Melissa almost choked with laughter. "Of course not, silly girl." She started to cough. Her eyes widened when she hacked up a button.

Allison recognized it from Joey's polo shirt.

She gasped.

"Okay, I might have eaten that one," Melissa admitted, "but only because he annoyed me, not because I had to." Two tentacles whipped out from behind her back and wrapped around Allison's waist. "You're starting to annoy me, too."

Allison caught a glimpse of the monster within the girl as the tentacles brought her in closer. Cthulhu might have been turned on by the sight of the real Melissa, but Allison wanted to scream, or vomit, or both.

"I just want everyone to be friends." Melissa softened her tone as she gazed at Allison. "Nobody else has to be eaten, or even inconvenienced. All I ask for is your happiness. What would make you happy, Allison? What is it you like?"

"Me!" Taylor shouted. Her voice sounded muffled but full of defiance as she kicked open the basement door.

Allison didn't have time to ask Taylor about the protective suit and gloves she wore. The angry blonde charged at Melissa and dumped a large container of a clear liquid all over the stunned girl.

Melissa howled in pain. Her skin began to burn and melt off like candle wax, revealing pulsating flesh of mottled browns and greens. A brighter green oozed from cracks and fissures in her exposed flesh as she convulsed.

Allison backed away. She gagged; her empty stomach produced only bile.

"We gotta go!"

Taylor grabbed Allison's hand and held on tight to pull her out of the basement and up the stairs.

"What *was* that?"

Allison leaned back against the locker room door.

"Melissa or the liquid I dumped on her head?" Taylor asked, shaking out her blond hair after she removed her suit.

"Both!" Allison threw up her hands.

"Well, Melissa was obviously an alien, and I snuck a big jug of hydrochloric acid out of the science lab."

"How did you know it would work?"

Taylor stared at her. "It's hydrochloric acid. Why wouldn't it work?" She opened a locker to thrust the suit and gloves into a duffel bag. "I need to sneak these back into the science lab tomorrow morning. Fortunately, I wore them in chemistry this week so it's fine if they test for DNA."

"Who *are* you?" Allison asked.

"*Not* an alien." Taylor's blue eyes sparkled. "I told you. I like winning." She grinned, throwing an arm around Allison's shoulder to plant a sloppy kiss on her cheek before she guided her out of the locker room.

A strange man with a buzz cut, dressed in a

nondescript black suit and dark sunglasses, looked up in surprise when they walked out. He pulled out some sort of high-tech baton and passed it over Taylor and Allison.

"What were you doing in there?"

"It's the girls' locker room," Taylor told him. She rolled her eyes, then treated him to her most haughty glare. "Wouldn't you like to know?"

"Well, you two better hurry home," the man said. "There's been reports of…of a potential shooter, and we're making sure the building is clear," he added.

"Whatever, weirdo."

Taylor led Allison away.

The man put away his baton as he watched the girls continue down the hall toward the exit.

"Everything okay in there, Charlie?" someone inquired over the walkie talkie clipped to his belt.

"Yeah, Oscar. Just sending out a couple of teen girls," he answered. "Still no signs of intelligent life." He laughed.

"They cute, though?" Oscar asked after a moment.

"They're teenagers," Charlie reminded him as he walked down the hallway, peering into different classrooms.

"Yeah, but are they cute?"

"I dunno," Charlie answered. "The blonde was hot, I guess."

"Yeah, I see her now." Oscar let out a low whistle. "If you still haven't found anything, might as well leave."

While Charlie considered asking if Oscar

wanted to detain the girls for more questioning, a tentacle snaked up the nearby stairwell before wrapping around his throat.

He gasped and reached for it, dropping the walkie talkie.

"What the hell was that?" shouted the voice of Oscar over the walkie talkie. "Charlie? Charlie!"

the fangover

Danielle Harris awoke with a groan. She pulled a plush blanket over her head as a ray of sunlight sneaked in through the blinds. She did not remember returning to her dorm room or crawling into bed last night, but she felt happy to be there. Or at least she would if not for the throbbing headache.

Another groan escaped Danielle when her smartphone beeped. "Who the hell is texting me so early?"

The digital clock on her phone said it was almost noon. The message had come from her best friend, Brian Wu: *Dani! WTF happened to you last night?*

"Hell if I know," she muttered to herself.

Danielle decided to take a shower before she replied. Maybe she would remember the answer to his question by then. She pushed herself up and out of bed with a grunt. She was not surprised she still had on last night's outfit, but she was surprised to see her roommate Megan still sleeping in the bed across from hers.

Weekend or not, Megan Miller was the type of girl to be up at the butt crack of dawn for a morning run, even on Sundays. By this time, she should be at brunch with her aggressively cheerful friends, not lazing about in bed.

Staying out at a dive bar, indulging in a late-night snack at a super sketchy diner, and sleeping in well past noon…that was more Danielle's style.

So why was Megan still asleep?

Danielle stumbled into the bathroom and turned the light on. She began to remove her clothing: a shimmery black halter top that Bryan had once described as a glorified handkerchief, dark blue skin-tight jeans, and a pair of barely-there black panties. Everything appeared to be in one piece, her body included, so she decided she must not have had too much fun last night.

Danielle stepped into the shower, closing her eyes as she allowed the hot water to pour all over her body. She adopted a relaxed pace as she washed her hot pink hair without bothering to clean up any of the pale pink splatters the semi-permanent dye left on the tiles. After rinsing, she squeezed the contents from one of Megan's neatly labeled bottles of body wash onto a sponge because she was out of her own soap.

Danielle remained in the shower until the water ran cold. She never took a shower before Megan in the morning. Danielle wondered how mad her roommate would be to awaken to a lack of hot water. The thought made her smile.

Danielle draped herself in her fluffy pink bath

sheet as she stepped out of the shower. She leaned over the sink to wipe the steam off the bathroom mirror even though she knew Megan hated when she did that. She did not see the way her forehead wrinkled in confusion as she looked in the mirror. It reflected only the towel rack behind her.

Danielle gasped. She slapped a hand over her mouth, hoping Megan did not hear her. She opened the bathroom door to look at the other girl's bed. Megan still slept, messy brown curls obscuring her pale face.

Danielle hurried to her dresser, dropping her wet towel on the floor. She pulled out a fresh pair of underwear, shorts, and a tank top. After she was dressed, Danielle returned to the bathroom.

Still no reflection.

Danielle tugged a comb through her wet tangles. She swept her hair up into a loose twist at the back of her head before securing it with a butterfly clip that she found on the counter. The clip may or may not have been hers. She became aware of an unpleasant sensation in her gums. Every nerve in every tooth throbbed.

Then something sharp poked her lower lip.

Two somethings, to be exact.

Danielle touched her mouth, and her fingers came away red with blood. She opened her mouth, feeling stupid as she ran her fingers along her teeth. Danielle's eyes widened as she felt her front canines. They were elongated.

"This is not happening," she told an empty mirror.

Danielle thought of Megan, still sound asleep in

the next room, even though it was now past noon. She left the bathroom, taking a few soft steps to stand beside her roommate's bed. Danielle struggled to see the rise and fall of Megan's chest. She brushed a lock of curly brown hair out of the girl's freckled face.

Nothing.

Her unease grew.

Danielle placed two fingers on the side of Megan's throat until she was able to detect a heartbeat. Her roommate stirred.

Anxious to leave the dorm room before Megan woke up, Danielle slipped her feet into a pair of her flip flops. She slid her smartphone into the back pocket of her shorts as she stepped onto the hall.

Danielle made a quick beeline for Bryan's room, hoping to find him alone. She was in luck. Bryan glanced at Danielle, his dark eyes quizzical behind his glasses as he paused his video game. He moved over to make a space for her on the edge of his unmade bed, but Danielle sat on his roommate's bed instead.

"Did Harry go home for the weekend again?"

Bryan nodded. "Are you going to tell me what happened last night? We tried to meet up with you at the Cellar, but someone said you'd already come and gone, and you didn't answer any of my texts."

Danielle frowned. "I didn't get any texts from you at all last night." She pulled her smartphone out of her pocket to double check. "This morning was the first text since yesterday afternoon."

"Why do you sound like you have a lisp?"

Danielle looked up and bared her fangs.

"Holy crap!" Bryan stood. "I've heard of people

getting misspelled tattoos or crazy piercings when they're wasted, but you're the first person I know who capped their teeth. What else did you do last night?"

"I didn't get my teeth capped."

Bryan knelt before her, adjusting his glasses. "May I?"

Danielle bared her teeth again. Bryan pressed against the tip of one of her canines. "It's retractable!"

"What?"

Danielle felt again for herself. The canine gave against her fingertip. She found that if she concentrated hard enough, she could make both fangs retract at will.

"So, what *did* you do last night?" Bryan sat back down.

"I don't remember," Danielle confessed. "I know I went to the Cellar to meet you, but there was someone else, and we talked, and I left, but I don't remember who I talked to, or where we went. It's all a total blur, and after that, nothing. Like, I don't even remember having any drinks yet. My memories are just...gone."

"Somebody must've seen who you left with last night." Bryan ran a hand through his already disheveled black hair. "I'll start retracing your steps."

"What about me?"

"You have fangs. You're not casting a reflection. That's probably why you haven't fixed your raccoon eyes from your eyeliner, and, well, you look a bit rough, no offense." Bryan rose, growing more agitated as he paced the room. "It's daytime. If you go out into the sun, you might burst into flames, or maybe you'll get all sparkly instead, and people will just think you went too hard at a rave or something, but I'd rather not take any chances."

Bryan stopped his pacing at the door. Then he turned to Danielle with a shaky grin. "Try not to eat anyone while I'm gone, okay...?"

Danielle frowned.

"What's wrong?" Bryan's grin faded.

"I'm hungry..."

Kimberly Zhao knocked on the door of her boyfriend's room, but he didn't answer. She tucked a strand of shiny black hair behind her ear before trying the door handle. It was unlocked. Kimberly stepped inside. She felt dismayed to see Danielle asleep in Bryan's bed, wearing one of his hoodies.

"What are you doing here? Where's Bryan?"

Danielle rubbed her eyes and sat up, blinking at Kimberly. "He went to the café, and he's letting me hang out because Megan's mad at me."

"What else is new?"

Kimberly sat down at Bryan's desk, turning the swivel chair around to face the bed.

Danielle did not make eye contact. Instead she sat with her head tilted to the side, her gaze settling on the neat curve where Kimberly's neck met her chest.

Kimberly looked down, examining her shirt and collar to see if something was wrong, but she noted nothing unusual. Still, the other girl stared, her expression vacant. "Why are you looking at me like that? And what's up with your face?"

Startled, Danielle made eye contact with

Kimberly. "Sorry. I must've fallen asleep with my eyes open or something. I had kind of a bad night."

"You look it," Kimberly replied.

Both girls looked at the doorway as Bryan walked into the room, holding a paper bag. He glanced between Danielle and Kimberly, alarmed. Then he opened the bag and tossed Danielle a wrapped burger. "It's as rare as they would make it."

Danielle ripped off the wrapper and devoured the burger in a few large bites. Juices ran down her chin. She licked her lips and wiped her chin with the back of her hand.

Kimberly watched Danielle in abject horror, wrinkling her nose. "Since when does she eat red meat?"

Bryan forced a nervous laugh. "You know college girls, always experimenting." He led Kimberly into the hall by her elbow, closing the door.

"So, what are you doing here?"

"We were supposed to meet up for lunch and go to the movies after." Kimberly frowned. "Did you forget?"

"No." Bryan put his hands on her shoulders. "I'm sorry, Kim, but some guy stole Dani's purse last night. I'm gonna help her get it back."

Kimberly shrugged off his hands. "Why doesn't she call campus security or the cops or whoever. What if he's dangerous?"

"I promise we'll go out tomorrow."

"I might be busy." Kimberly blinked back tears. She turned and walked quickly down the hall. Bryan watched her go, frowning, before he went back into his room.

Danielle looked up, licking her fingers clean.

Bryan struggled to conceal his disgust, his lips twitching. "I found out more information about your guy, but nobody there last night knew where you were going."

"Who was he?"

"Some guy with a buzz cut in leather pants and a tank top. Tall. Muscular."

"Just my type. Doesn't really narrow it down, does it?"

"There's something else. People told me that he had this weird tattoo on his neck." Bryan paused for effect. "A butterfly."

"*That's* different." Danielle raised her eyebrows.

Bryan nodded. "I thought so, too. I asked around, found out it has something to do with a new club downtown."

Danielle rose. "Does this club have a name?"

"Metamorphosis."

A taxi dropped Danielle and Bryan off at the club downtown. She was dressed in another slinky black top and dark jeans, with Bryan's assurance that her makeup looked okay, if a little more rock-and-roll than usual. Bryan wore contacts instead of his glasses, as well as a muscle tee, jeans, and a wallet chain Danielle had kept from one of her ex-boyfriends.

He looked at the other people in line. Some appeared rough and even a little scary; others dressed in more stylish attire but retained a hard edge to their looks and demeanor.

"I don't even *have* a motorcycle," Bryan muttered

under his breath.

"They don't know that," Danielle reassured him. "Just act natural. I mean, don't act. Just be cool. But naturally."

Bryan raised his eyebrows.

They reached the front of the line. The bouncer, a large man whose black tee revealed far more impressive muscles than the ones possessed by the shorter, lankier Bryan, gave a gruff nod in Danielle's direction. She started to enter the club, but the bouncer held out a hand to stop Bryan. "Not you."

Danielle looked at him with a helpless shrug.

"Don't go without me," Bryan pleaded.

"I have to get answers."

"What if something else happens?"

"In or out?" the bouncer barked at Danielle.

She lowered her eyes.

"In."

Danielle turned away from Bryan without saying another word. His scowl deepened as he watched her disappear into the hazy glow.

Inside the club, people danced to pulsing electronic music or mingled in booths along the perimeter of the dance floor. Danielle walked up to the bar. She flagged a bartender, a slim attractive man with dark spiky hair.

"Do you remember seeing me last night?" Danielle struggled to make herself heard over the music. "I might have come in with a big tough guy?"

The bartender cupped his hands over his ears and shook his head. "What do you want to drink?" he shouted back.

"Long Island iced tea," Danielle carefully enunciated.

She hoped that the bartender could read her lips better than he could hear. The bartender returned with her drink. She paid for it with cash out of her back pocket, feeling a twinge of guilt that Bryan had loaned her the money. Danielle turned and leaned back against the bar. She scanned the crowd, drinking her Long Island through the straw. To her relief it tasted alright, even if the ache in her teeth reminded her that she craved something more.

Danielle felt her hips start to move to the current song's throbbing baseline. She removed the straw and downed her drink before setting the empty glass on the bar. Then she pushed through the crowd until she found a spot to dance in earnest.

A middle-aged man in a rumpled sports coat grabbed her arm and whispered in her ear, "I have a VIP booth. You wanna sit with me?" His breath reeked of alcohol and onions.

"Pass." Danielle shrugged him off.

His grip tightened as he tried to pull her off the dance floor.

"Hard pass!"

Danielle pulled her wrist free and shoved him. The man flew backward and slid across the floor, hitting his head on a table leg. He appeared to groan as he sank to the floor with his eyes closed, but she could not hear him over the music. Danielle looked down at her hands. She raised her head, grinning.

"Did anyone see that?"

Only two stony-faced bouncers had taken notice, scowling as they strode across the club. Other people stepped around the downed man as if he was not even there. They paid little attention to Danielle, or the bouncers, as they continued to dance.

"Hey! He started it!"

Large hands grabbed either shoulder to steer Danielle out of the club. She felt confident she could shake them off, but then she remembered her reason for being at the club in the first place. After the bouncers shoved her out the back door, Danielle pulled her phone out of her pocket to text Bryan.

Total waste of time. All five minutes of it.

She waited, but he didn't reply.

When Danielle returned to Bryan's room, she found Kimberly alone, sitting on his bed. The girl rose to confront her.

"Where is he?"

Danielle's eyes widened. "He didn't come back?"

"He's supposed to be with you, and he isn't answering any of my texts." Kimberly folded her arms across her chest, still glaring at Danielle. "He wouldn't be the first coed to disappear under unusual circumstances."

Danielle recalled seeing posters for missing students. Wondering if there was some sort of connection to her present dilemma, she shuddered. "He couldn't get past the bouncer at this club we went to, so I had to go inside without him," Danielle said aloud. "It's only been a few hours."

Kimberly looked taken aback. Then her cheeks flushed with anger. "The whole reason he blew me off was to help you, and you just went in without him anyway?" She shook her head. "God, Dani. Why are you always so selfish?"

"I...I don't know. I just didn't think."

Kim unfolded her arms and strode to Danielle. "That's just it! You never think. It's your world. The rest of us just live in it."

"I...I'm sorry." Danielle left the room.

Danielle opened the door to her own room. She saw Megan and a couple of friends watching a TV show on Megan's computer, eating popcorn. They looked up.

Megan glared at Danielle. "Is that my shirt?"

Danielle shut the door and walked away.

Danielle sat on a bench outside the dorm. Nobody else was around. The last people she had seen were a couple of drunk, giggling girls returning to the dorm from a night out. She thought of Megan and her friends, wishing she had a friend or two of her own. Bryan was nice and all, but there was something to be said for female companionship.

Bryan.

Danielle sent him another text.

Where are you?

No answer.

She never heard so much as a footstep before her world went dark. Danielle tried to reach up for the heavy fabric her mysterious assailant had pulled down over her head, but strong hands grabbed either arm to lift her from the bench and carry her away with ease. Make that two assailants. The fabric muffled her grunts and screams as she tried in vain to escape. Her newfound strength failed her as they deposited her in the trunk of a car.

Danielle's heart sank as her dark world grew even darker.

Someone removed the hood after a long drive and a short trip up a flight of stairs. Danielle blinked, rubbing her eyes. The warm, humid air smelled sweet and pungent. A cursory glance at all the plants and the glass walls confirmed she was sitting in a greenhouse.

A beautiful woman with silky auburn hair and amber eyes sat across from Danielle. She wore stiletto heels and a velvety strapless dress in a rich shade of crimson that hugged her curves. Her ruby red lips curled into a sly smile.

Danielle heard a moan of pain, but it did not come from the woman. She looked down at her feet and gasped. An unconscious Bryan lay crumpled on the ground before her, a puddle of blood pooling beside his head. The goose egg and darkening bruise on his temple suggested someone had struck him so hard, the skin had split open. If there was any internal bleeding or swelling, the wound could be fatal.

"Oh, Dani, don't you worry about him. Not yet." The woman's melodic voice poured over Danielle like honey. "It's so nice to see you again." She smiled, her red lips parting to reveal fangs.

Danielle looked away from Bryan. "Who are you?"

"I would rather talk about who you are…and who you have the potential to be." The woman extended a hand, showing off her long but perfectly manicured red nails.

"Looks like I have all the time in the world to figure that out for myself," Danielle said. She peered out the glass windows of the greenhouse but saw only darkness.

The woman's eyes flashed with irritation. "Don't get ahead of yourself. You're not fully transformed until your first kill." She gestured to Bryan.

Danielle shuddered at the implication but forced herself to return the woman's cold stare. "If I kill you instead, will it cure me?"

Somehow the woman came to be standing behind the chair, though Danielle never saw her move. She shivered as a slender hand caressed her cheek. Then the woman grabbed her chin and forehead as if to snap her neck. "You can't kill me, and I can tear you apart in an instant if you're stupid enough to try anything."

The woman released her head. Danielle's hands flew to her throat, but the woman seized her wrists. "Or slowly, if I decide to take my time." She lifted one of Danielle's hands to her mouth, wrapping her lips around the pinkie finger.

First Danielle felt her wet but velvety tongue.

Then the vampire bit, hard.

She screamed.

The vampire laughed. She removed the severed finger from her mouth and tossed it back over her shoulder into a potted plant. "Now. You have a choice." She knelt in front of Danielle, grasping her chin. "Either you finish him off and my boys release you before dawn, or you stay here and burn."

Bryan groaned as the vampire released Danielle's chin.

"I think my boys may have been a little too rough with your friend, so he'll probably be dead before dawn anyway." The vampire nudged Bryan's side with one of her stilettoed feet. "No reason for you to die, too." She nodded at a security camera. "I'll be watching. Don't even think about calling for help or trying to leave on your own. I have friends everywhere."

Danielle sat cross-legged on the floor of the greenhouse as she cradled Bryan's head in her lap. The blood on his temple had mostly dried, dulling its effect on her hunger. She stared down at him in dismay as she brushed her fingers through his hair.

"She's right, you know," Bryan rasped.

Her relief to hear his voice faded when she realized what he meant.

"I am not killing my best friend," Danielle told him. "I may be an asshole, but I am not a monster. Not yet anyway. Besides, I've already been living like there's no tomorrow. Maybe there shouldn't be."

Bryan opened his eyes to stare at her. "What happened to you isn't your fault."

"That's the problem with kids these days. Nobody believes in personal accountability." The laugh that followed sounded more bitter than Danielle had intended.

"If you drink too much, you're responsible for that, but you're not responsible for what someone else does to you when you're drunk. That's on them."

"Maybe, but what happened to you is on me." She continued to stroke his hair tenderly as Bryan closed his eyes. "I should have said yes."

"What?"

"When you asked me out. I should have said yes."

"No. You didn't need a boyfriend. You needed a friend. And I...I love Kim. I haven't told her yet, but I do..." His voice trailed off.

Danielle looked at him, stricken.

Bryan lay on the floor, alone, as sunlight streamed into the greenhouse. He awoke with a groan, forcing himself up into a sitting position. He looked around the greenhouse but saw no sign of Danielle, not even a pile of ash.

A door opened behind Bryan. He turned to face the newcomer, wincing in pain.

Danielle grinned. She had wrapped her wounded hand, which she clutched to her chest, with a torn piece of black cloth. He stared up at her, amazed.

"I know, right? No flames. No sparkly skin. No more fangs." Her smile widened. "Can you believe it? I guess it's only temporary so long as you don't kill anyone."

Danielle tossed Bryan his smartphone with her good hand. He managed to catch it as he gazed at her in wonder.

"Anyway, Kim sent, like, a million texts. It's a good thing you're hurt because she says she's going to kill you if you're not already dead."

Bryan continued to stare at Danielle. Then he shook himself out of his daze. "You and I are going to have a serious talk about setting some personal boundaries if we get out of this alive, among other things."

"I know." Danielle gave Bryan a rueful grin. "I also owe you back for last night. Oh, and whatever the burger cost."

"Well, well, well. That was a first." The disembodied drawl of a woman interrupted them. Startled, Danielle and Bryan scanned the greenhouse until they identified the source of the voice: a speaker below a security camera.

"I admit I'm a little disappointed, but I like that humans can still surprise me after all this time. You're made of stronger stuff than I expected, Danielle."

Danielle and Bryan exchanged a worried glance.

"However, as illuminating as I have found this experiment to be, I'm starting to lose interest. I suggest the both of you leave before my appetite returns. I'll be keeping my eye on you, Danielle. Remember, I have friends everywhere."

Danielle helped Bryan to his feet.

"You really think she's gonna let us out of here alive?"

"For now." Danielle shrugged. "I think it's a game to her."

"Sounds like she isn't done playing with you."

"Guess I'll have to take things one day at a time." Danielle gave Bryan a shaky smile. "I really am sorry. For everything." He did not return it. She turned from him to face an uncertain future as they stepped into the sunshine.

ghosted

Blake Johnson: hey
　　　we set for next Sat?
Jennifer Rose: yes
limo company called Erin 2 confirm
Blake Johnson: kk
May 5, 4:05 PM

Kevin Mann: hey Jenny
started calc homework yet?
Jennifer Rose: nah, not yet
Kevin Mann: thought maybe you could
come over
I can help
Jennifer Rose: aww thanks, but it looks easy
Kevin Mann: oh, k
May 5, 4:27 P.M.

Amaya Rivera: hey
time 2 watch my presentation?

Jennifer Rose: dinner, can I call you after?
Amaya Rivera: k, thanks! ❤
May 5, 5:54 P.M.

Kevin Mann: hey Jenny
there's something else I wanted to ask u
I know it's short notice but do u want 2 go 2
prom?
May 5, 8:30 P.M.

Kevin Mann: just as friends 4 old time's sake
May 5, 8:41 PM

Kevin Mann: no pressure or anything
Jennifer Rose: already have plans but thanks
for thinking of me
hey u know who might be available?
Madeline Stuart
Kevin Mann: eh, she's not really my type
Jennifer Rose: she's so cute though
I think she likes you
May 5, 9:45 P.M.

Cody James: hey, u still awake?
Jennifer Rose: yeah, finishing homework
Cody James: so Blake wants to know if I
wanna get matching ties & cummerbunds
TF is a cummerbund?
Jennifer Rose: google is your friend
Cody James: sounds dirty
I don't wanna get grounded b4 prom
Jennifer Rose: omigod, CJ!
It's just a fabric thing that goes around ur

waist when u wear a tux
Cody James: oh, wow...
I was way off
Jennifer Rose: night CJ 🖤
May 5, 10:45 PM

Jennifer Rose: where r u?
Amaya Rivera: sorry
showing new guy to café
BRT
May 6, 11:30 AM

Jennifer Rose: he's cute!
He's in 2 of my classes
Amaya Rivera: someone said his old hs
expelled him 4 fighting
Jennifer Rose: he seems 2 chill 4 that
Amaya Rivera: gtg mrs m's watching
May 6, 1:30 PM

Kevin Mann: not 2 b nosy but ur going 2
prom w/Blake?!
Jennifer Rose: & CJ, Amaya
Kevin Mann: ah, gotcha
May 6, 7:35 PM

Kevin Mann: does this mean it's okay if I ask
u 2 dance?
Jennifer Rose: ur going?
did u ask Maddie?
Kevin Mann: nah
I'm keeping my options open
Jennifer Rose: cool

gotta finish essay
May 6, 8:10 PM

Amaya Rivera: do u wanna go dress
shopping after school?
or 2morrow?
Jennifer Rose: 2morrow
v tired
u wanna stay over tonight?
I just wanna silence my phone & hang
w/my bestie
Amaya Rivera: works 4 me
May 7, 1:24 PM

Kevin Mann: u there? everything ok?
May 8, 4:32 PM

Nicholas Cruz: hey
thanks 4 friend invite
Amaya Rivera: u should add Jennifer
she's my BFF
Nicholas Cruz: brunette, glasses?
we got English & SH together
Amaya Rivera: she may have mentioned
that
May 9, 7:38 PM

Jennifer Rose: the new guy sent me a friend
invite
Amaya Rivera: did u accept?
Jennifer Rose: obvsly
May 9, 8:46 PM

Jennifer Rose: I'm fine, just super busy
Kevin Mann: k I won't bug ya
May 9, 9:15 PM

Amaya Rivera: invited Nick 2 lunch
Jennifer Rose: r u up 2 something?
Amaya Rivera:
May 10, 10:20 AM

Kevin Mann: I noticed u & Amaya were
hanging out with the new guy
I've heard some bad things about him
May 10, 7:46 PM

Jennifer Rose: I already heard Nick's side
I don't care about gossip
Kevin Mann: k
I'm just looking out for ya
Jennifer Rose: thanks, night
May 10, 9:10 PM

Jennifer Rose: everything okay?
u looked kind of down when u got back from
guidance
Nicholas Cruz: my parent's lawyer called
u know that guy I told u about?
his family's still threatening 2 sue us
Jennifer Rose: I'm sorry 2 hear that
Nicholas Cruz: I never should've shoved him
so hard
I just got so angry
May 11, 6:24 PM

Amaya Rivera: 4got I still have history HM
u should go to lunch w/out me 2day
Jennifer Rose: srsly?
Amaya Rivera:
May 12, 11:27 AM

Kevin Mann: hey Jenny
u never did say if you'd dance w/me at prom
May 12, 6:48 PM

Jennifer Rose: thanks again 4 lunch
Nicholas Cruz: no prob
Jennifer Rose: there's a bonfire after prom
 on Sat
u should go
Nicholas Cruz: yeah
I might even go 2 prom
Nicholas Cruz: it sucks I have 2 miss my
own prom
u know what I mean
Jennifer Rose: did u have a date?
maybe u can bring her 2 ours
Nicholas Cruz: nah
I was just gonna go w/some friends
Jennifer Rose: oh
May 12, 8:30 PM

Kevin Mann:
May 12, 8:49 PM

Cody James: should I dye hair aqua to match
 bow & cummerbund?
Jennifer Rose: my heart says yes but my

mind says Blake will freak
Cody James: ur right
I'll do fuchsia instead
Jennifer Rose: dude
Cody James: jk
May 13, 6:53 PM

Blake Johnson: hey
we going to the bonfire after prom?
Jennifer Rose: yeah
limo's dropping us back off at Amaya's
I'll drive from there
May 14, 5:28 PM

Cody James: ur boy is here
he just danced with Maddie
what r u 2 doin in there?
Jennifer Rose: Aww
my zipper got stuck
May 15, 7:35 PM

Amaya Rivera: sorry 2 interrupt but limo's
here
he's going 2 bonfire, right?
Jennifer Rose: Yes
May 15, 9:48 PM

Nicholas Cruz: where r u at?
Jennifer Rose: pavilion b
May 15, 10:56 PM

Jennifer Rose: we're going for a walk on the
beach

back soon
Amaya Rivera:
May 15, 11:43 PM

Nicholas Cruz: where r u?
have u seen Jenny?
Amaya Rivera: I'm by the bonfire
I thought she was w/u
Nicholas Cruz: she was
someone kept calling her
she told me 2 go back & she'd catch up with me
Amaya Rivera: u left her?
Nicholas Cruz: no
she left me but didn't say where she was going
thought u were the one calling in case she
needed an excuse 2 go
but everything seemed cool before then
now I'm just worried
Amaya Rivera: same
meet me at bonfire
May 16, 12:30 AM

Amaya Rivera: have u seen Jenny?
Blake Johnson: no
I saw her go off w/Nick
Amaya Rivera: he's with me now
We can't find her
Blake Johnson: we'll check pier
Stick to the crowd, k?
Amaya Rivera: ???
May 16, 12:37 AM

Cody James: still haven't found her?

Blake might call his mom
Amaya Rivera: no
I was hoping it wouldn't come 2 that
Cody James: Nick doesn't know where she went?
he's the last person who saw her
Amaya Rivera: I know...
May 16, 1:20 AM

Jennifer Rose: . . .
Kevin Mann: Jenny?
Jennifer Rose: . . .
May 16, 1:35 AM

Kevin Mann: r u trying 2 reach me?
Jennifer Rose: . . .
May 16, 2:10 AM

Kevin Mann: Jenny, ur scaring me
Jennifer Rose: . . .
May 16, 3:34 AM

Kevin Mann: did something happen last night?
There's cops at Jenny's house
I see Blake's mom
Amaya Rivera: she disappeared @ bonfire
Kevin Mann: weren't u 2gether?
Amaya Rivera: we got separated
I can't talk now
v tired & worried
May 16, 9:10 AM

Kevin Mann: Amaya
he did something to her
the new guy
May 16, 9:31 AM

Kevin Mann: why did u let her go off w/him
alone?
u heard the stories
Amaya Rivera: Nick got expelled 4
defending a freshman girl from a bully
0-tolerance policy
May 16, 9:58 AM

Amaya Rivera: hold up
I didn't see u last night
how did u know she was w/Nick?
Kevin?
May 16, 10:15 AM

Kevin Mann: I think she's been trying 2
message me
looks like she's still in the middle of typing
something but she never hits send
it's just those three dots
weird, right?
Amaya Rivera: yah I guess
but how did you know she was w/Nick?
May 16, 10:48 AM

Kevin Mann: people talk
May 16, 11:07 AM

Kevin Mann: the dots went away

May 16, 11:32 AM
Amaya Rivera: have u heard anything else?
Blake Johnson: cops found a phone on the beach
by the pier
May 16, 12:01 PM

Kevin Mann: hey
you know what?
I bet Nick took her phone and he's messing with me
Amaya Rivera: ...
May 16, 12:20 PM

Blake Johnson: overheard dad on phone w/mom
sounds like they found Jenny
Amaya Rivera: where was she?
is she okay?
Blake Johnson: can I call?
May 16, 2:18 PM

Kevin Mann: Amaya?
What were you gonna say?
May 16, 2:35 PM

Nicholas Cruz: Amaya?
Amaya Rivera: she's gone
Nicholas Cruz: I know
police were here a little while ago
they just had a few questions
Amaya Rivera: oh
Nicholas Cruz: I want u 2 know that I'd never

do anything 2 hurt Jenny
never should've let her go
May 16, 3:56 PM

Amaya Rivera: is there a way I can reach ur mom?
Blake Johnson: she just talked 2 Cody should b contacting u next
Amaya Rivera: good
May 16, 4:16 PM

Kevin Mann: the cops r back
May 16, 6:24 PM

Amaya Rivera: she was still alive when she fell in the water
did u know that?
I heard it on the news
May 17, 6:47 PM

Amaya Rivera: there were bruises on her arms & her neck, but she was alive when she fell
Amaya Rivera: how could u?
May 17, 6:55 PM

Blake Johnson sent you a <u>link</u>.
June 2, 3:50 PM

"Update in Prom Night Tragedy"
June 2

Pictured: J. Rose and classmate

Local residents are still reeling from the devastating news that high school senior Kevin Mann, 18, has been arrested in connection with the homicide of Jennifer Rose, 18, at a bonfire following their senior prom last month. Sources say text messages, phone records, and DNA evidence confirm K. Mann's involvement.

Residents say K. Mann and J. Rose had been close friends since kindergarten. According to one neighbor, "Kevin seemed like such a nice boy. Just goes to show, girls can never be too careful nowadays." Another neighbor describes the young man's appearance as "haunted", saying "whether it's from guilt or grief, who's to say?"

Specific charges are pending.

omega

The moon hung low over the forest.

A squirrel foraged for nuts and seeds before darting up an oak tree. It chattered a warning to the other squirrels as it cast furtive glances at the forest floor below.

A fox sat back on its haunches, glaring at the dried leaves that betrayed its presence. Then it dove for a hole in a rotting tree trunk as something much larger lumbered through the underbrush .

The hulking beast sniffed at the crisp night air. It could smell everything from the musk of a nearby skunk to the tang of newly ripened berries. Its nose twitched as it detected two scents less common to its forest home: something sweet and muted and lovely, and something more pungent and cloying, both masking the distinct odor of humans.

It rose to its full height on powerful hind legs and pushed through the dense underbrush until it reached a parking lot. Grasping the trunk of an ancient oak tree broad enough to conceal its wide frame, the beast peered out from behind it. The sounds of a struggle emanated from a nearby vehicle.

The beast dropped to all fours, moving closer to the coupe. Inside, a teenage girl shrieked, and a teenage boy grunted. The beast crouched lower to the ground as the passenger door opened. A large shape fell out in a heap.

"I said 'no!'"

"You broke my nose!" the boy growled at the girl in the car as he pushed himself into a sitting position, only it sounded more like he had said *bose.* He clutched at his ruined face, blood pouring from between his fingers.

Though it had yet to taste human flesh, the hungry beast licked its lips in anticipation. It rose once more, standing at well over six feet of solid muscle. Its hulking frame cast a formidable shadow as it emerged from behind the tree to roar at the boy. The boy let go of his nose, his eyes round with terror as he scrambled to his feet.

The beast prepared to leap as the frightened boy turned to run, but the driver's side door opened. "No, no. It's okay, Duke," the girl said as she stepped out of the car. "I got this." She glared at the back of the boy, who had taken advantage of this moment to make a break for it. "Have a nice run home, you creep!"

Duke sat back on his haunches and stared, his orange eyes puzzled as he tilted his broad head. The girl was small but solid with brown hair pulled back in a messy ponytail. A familiar image of a bird in flight adorned her shirt.

"Duke. That is your name, isn't it?"

Unafraid, the girl sat down on a wooden stump

beside Duke. "At least I think that's the name Sara told the team she gave you. You do have sort of a regal air about you, but I think I would have gone with an even better name. Like Prince. I'm Amanda." She scratched the beast behind one of his ears.

Duke released a soft whimper in response to her touch as he leaned into it. With a hopeful sidelong glance, he placed a furry paw on her thigh.

"No, Duke."

Amanda pushed his paw off her leg as she gave Duke a gentle look of reproach.

Duke whimpered an apology.

"Oh, Duke," she sighed. "You get it. Why didn't he?"

Amanda leaned her head against his shoulder. After a few moments, she rose to her feet. "It's a good thing I'm not in any hurry to have a boyfriend. You must get lonely, though. I hope there's someone... well, something, out there for you. You can't be the only one of your kind. G'night, Duke."

Duke watched her go, his already long face made even longer by morose. With a heavy sigh, he rose and began to lumber down the road, keeping close to the tree line.

Duke tried to avoid the residential areas, but something always drew him to this street. It was many blocks away from the other girl, the one with yellow hair who sometimes brought him bones to gnaw on. One side of the road was still densely forested. Duke kept to the shadows on that side as he gazed at the row of modest houses across the street.

The gentle fragrance of lavender and honey

wafted by Duke's nose. His ears and even the small deer-like tail between his hind legs twitched with curiosity. He stared at one of the homes, a small yellow cottage with a white roof and a wraparound porch. Like the home of the yellow-haired girl, a wooden swing hung from the roof.

On this swing there sat a woman with lined eyes and graying hair, dressed in light blue nursing scrubs. She looked as sad and despondent as Duke felt. He moved back further as the front door of the house opened.

"Honey, why don't you come inside?" a man said. "I've fixed you a sandwich."

As she rose from the porch swing, the woman gazed into the forest across the road. For a moment, Duke thought her sad eyes fell upon him, even as he crouched low in the shadows amid the trees. The woman stared for another moment. Then she turned to walk inside the house, closing the door.

Despite his heavy fur, Duke grew colder. He refrained from howling in the misery he felt.

Instead of returning home to his den in the forest, Duke ambled down the street, deeper into residential areas and past a couple of strip malls. He stopped at a small but well-cared-for garden nestled between two roads perpendicular to the main street.

A tall sign stood in the center of the garden. Though Duke was unable to read it, something about the image of a proud antlered stag felt familiar to him, and not just because he had seen the occasional deer in the woods before they darted in the opposite direction. He also remembered the bird on

Amanda's shirt.

As Duke hid himself in the shadows, a few cars drove on or off the main road. He waited for a lull in traffic to cross the first of the smaller roads. Then he followed the second road, still sticking close to the trees.

Large buildings sprawled before him. All but one in the center of a grassy lawn were dark. Duke darted for cover behind a tree here or a lamppost there to take a closer look.

The lamppost proved to be a poor hiding spot.

"Woah!" A young man with long sandy blond hair gaped at him. "Cool costume, dude!" He clapped Duke on the back and continued walking.

"I didn't think those weirdos came out on Karaoke night."

The man's red-haired companion looked back over her shoulder at Duke, a look of disdain marring her otherwise pretty face.

"Live and let live," the man told her.

Duke followed the couple at a distance. He glanced down at his raggedy pants, feeling a distant sense of shame. A small group of young adults stared as Duke ducked under an archway to enter the building. With a toothy grin and a rueful shrug of his broad shoulders, he lumbered past them to a nearby stairwell.

His ears perked at the sound of music and laughter, muffled by a pair of heavy oak doors at the bottom and to the left of the stairwell.

"Now that's something you don't see every day." Dave stared at the Cellar's stage, his brown eyes dazed as he scratched at his ear.

Natalie began to restock the cups, lids, and straws she had brought from the back room of the coffee kiosk. "Yeah, nobody's ever mumbled their way through 'Creep' before," she muttered.

Natalie did not look up until the chorus. Her jaw dropped.

A large hulking beast with a wolfish face and spiraling horns, like those of a ram, on either side of its furry head howled in tune with the song. It wore only a pair of ragged jeans.

"That's the most amazing costume I've ever seen," Dave told Natalie. "I don't see any of his buddies around, though. I thought they only came out on game night."

"I don't think that's a costume," Natalie said, eyes wide.

"Nee's uhnning ahwayayayaooo!" the beast warbled on stage. As it howled the song to its completion, the audience stared, first at each other, then the beast. They erupted into thunderous applause and shouts and whistles.

A young woman with kohl-lined pale blue eyes and dark curls cascading down her back watched from a small table as the beast lumbered out of the Cellar, her ruby red lips forming an 'oh' of surprise. As the next performer took the stage, she rose from her seat and followed the beast outside.

Duke's heart had swollen with pride and longing after his impromptu performance inside the building. Now, as he curled up in the shadow of a large oak tree on the lawn, he felt only the dull pang of loneliness. He rested his head on his large paws, his eyes closing.

"Hey you," a soft voice said.

Duke opened one eye. A young raven-haired woman knelt on the grass beside him. She wore a black low-cut sweater and a knee-length denim skirt. The shiny red of her lips and nails matched the red stone dangling from the black velvet choker at her throat.

"You don't know me, but I think I might know who you are." She put her hand on the side of his face, stroking the fur. "I can help you."

Duke opened his other eye. He pushed himself up with a loud harrumph.

The young woman rose as well.

"Come on."

The woman led Duke to a black coupe in a parking lot. She gave him a look of appraisal as she considered the vehicle.

"Hmm. This might be a tight fit."

The woman opened the passenger door and adjusted the seat as far back as it would go to make room for Duke's legs, but he still had to hunch over. "Don't worry about that," the woman assured him as one of his horns punctured the inside of the car.

After a short drive, the woman parked in the driveway of a split-level home. She led Duke up the stairs to the apartment on the second floor. It consisted of a small living room, kitchen, and master suite.

Duke looked at the flimsy black futon against a wall in the living room. Plush red and purple throw pillows added the only dash of color to the sparse room. It was otherwise empty apart from the framed print on the wall depicting a human skull surrounded by roses. A flat-screen TV stood on a stand across from the futon.

Instead of the futon in the living room, the woman led Duke to the bed in the bedroom. Duke raised a bushy eyebrow and mewled.

"I can help you," the woman explained, "but you might want to lie down."

His eyes narrowing, Duke watched her as he laid down atop the black velvet comforter. Though she slept in a king-sized bed, his massive cloven feet stuck out past the edge.

The woman bit her lip on a smile as she turned from Duke to sort through a strange pile of trinkets and potions on her cherry wood vanity. She sat on the velvet cushioned stool, absorbed in her work as he watched from the bed.

Duke could not see what the woman was doing as she began to chant under her breath, but mysterious tendrils of green smoke began to fill the room. The pungent fumes stung his eyes. Tears ran down Duke's cheeks as a strange tingling sensation spread from his spine into his extremities and even his jaws.

The chanting rose in volume and intensity.

Duke felt his body rise from the bed. He gasped and writhed as the tingling sensation was replaced by fiery searing pain. It felt as though every bone in his body was straining to get away from every other bone even as they condensed beneath his tightening skin. Even his skull felt like it was about to explode, implode, or both. He threw his head back and howled in agony and despair.

Then, as soon as it had begun, everything went still.

Duke fell back with greater awareness of the velvet comforter against his skin. He did not know how much time had passed before the bed gave a little under the weight of the woman. She knelt beside him, holding a warm washcloth against his forehead as she gazed down at him with a look of intense affection.

"Jake?"

Her voice had grown less sultry, more tentative yet tender.

"Is that your name?"

Duke...no, Jake sat up with a start, reaching to pull the wet cloth from his skin. Not fur but skin. "How did you...who are you?"

He stared at the woman as he reached up to touch his face, feeling only a hint of stubble as his hands moved up his square jaw to find high chiseled cheekbones, then traced an aquiline nose. Now he ran his fingers through the hair on his head and found no trace of the ram-like horns that had once weighed down his head and his spirits.

"My name is Brianna. I don't know you, but I saw the posters all over campus." Her pale blue eyes regarded him from under dark heavy lashes as she toyed with the jewel at her throat. "I...you look just like him."

Jake rose from the bed, buttoning a torn and ragged pair of what had once been jeans. He looked at his reflection in the vanity mirror. A slender but muscular young man of average height with light brown hair and brown eyes stared back at him. Then he looked down at the vanity and the odd assortment of vials, crystals, and more questionable items.

Was that a bird's foot?

He turned back to Brianna.

"Did you do it to me? Turn me into that thing?"

"I didn't mean to," she confessed in a small voice. "I must've snuck in the wrong shower stall in the men's locker room at the gym, or taken the wrong strand of hair, or something." Brianna shook her head, lost in thought. "I had a feeling it was too light to be his."

Jake's expression darkened. "How long have you known?"

Brianna blinked at his change in tone. "Not until I saw you tonight at the Cellar. I mean, a part of me always worried your disappearance had something to do with what I'd done, the timing and all, but I didn't know for sure until I read your aura." She looked at him with a coy smile as she twirled a strand of black hair around her index finger. "You know," she purred, "maybe all of this happened for a reason."

Brianna rose from the bed and walked to Jake. She placed one of her hands on his back, tracing the bare skin with her long red nails, resting her other hand on his chest. "I was so angry. I wanted to make him pay for using me. Instead, I found you." Her hand moved up to play with the hair at the back of his neck as she gazed into his eyes. "Like some higher power brought us together." She leaned in closer to nuzzle him.

Jake pulled away from Brianna. "You're crazy."

Her eyes narrowed. "I could make you love me."

"Yeah, there's a word for that."

Jake pushed past her. He ran out of the apartment without looking back. He could only hope he didn't leave behind any stray hairs.

The gravel hurt his bare feet, but Jake ran until he reached the main street. Some vehicles slowed as they passed him. People honked their horns or rolled down their windows to whistle and jeer at him, but nobody stopped. Jake continued to walk in misery, his head low.

Natalie left work after the karaoke crowd tapered off. When the car ahead of hers slowed to a crawl, she assumed they were braking for a deer or a dog. Instead she heard shouting and laughter. Up ahead, Natalie saw the real cause of the commotion. A young man wearing only denim cutoffs walked along the sidewalk, hunched over with his head down.

"Wow. That's a fir...well, second, actually," Natalie murmured. She tried not to stare as she drove past, but she saw the man sigh out of the corner of her eye. She slowed to a stop next to the sidewalk, lowering her passenger side window.

The man appeared wary as he approached. Natalie gasped when he looked into the window. "Oh, wow. You're Jake Mills, aren't you? I see your picture every day at work. You've been missing for almost a year. Do you need a ride to the hospital or the police station or something?" She unlocked the door.

Jake reached for the handle but paused. "Actually, there's somewhere else I'd like to go first, if that's okay."

When Natalie nodded, he opened the door and sat down.

Natalie cast a sidelong glance at Jake's bare torso. "Uhm, I have an extra sweatshirt in the backseat, if you want. It belonged to my ex. It might be a bit big on you," she added, her tone apologetic. "He's a football player."

Jake turned to look at the backseat. He reached for a large gray sweatshirt with a picture of a stag: the college mascot, he now remembered. Instead of masculine and musky, the sweatshirt smelled of the same delicate perfume Natalie wore. He gave her a grateful smile before he pulled it down over his head. Then he buckled his seatbelt.

"So, Jake, where to?"

Natalie pulled into the driveway of a small cottage with a wraparound porch and wooden swing.

"Wait for me?" Jake asked.

"Of course."

Jake walked up the steps of the porch to the front door. He started to knock but hesitated, looking back at Natalie. She nodded at him with an encouraging smile.

Jake knocked.

After a minute or an eternity, the door opened.

"Hi, Mom."

Natalie watched as the door opened and a woman dressed in scrubs took Jake into her arms. A man hung back for a few moments before joining in the embrace.

Natalie smiled. She would wait as long as they needed.

acknowledgments

Thank you to Michael, my biggest cheerleader and toughest critic (second only to myself) for loving and supporting me, even when I'm a bit of a monster myself. Especially that bleary eyed terror that emerged after nights when inspiration struck a little too late.

Thank you to my favorite little monsters Dieter and Xander for keeping yourselves entertained and (mostly) out of trouble when I was sleeping in after those late night writing sessions; and to the occasionally silly but never monstrous Alexandra, just for being you.

Thank you to my parents and mother-in-law for your support and encouragement.

Thank you to Writing Bloc for believing in me. Particular thanks go to my editor Cari Dubiel for all your immeasurable guidance and support; and to G.A. Finocchiaro for ensuring the cover art completed my vision.

Thank you to every creator whose work touched and inspired me, and made me feel less alone. The arts matter. You matter.

Thank you, readers. In case you need the reminder, you matter, too.

about writing bloc

Writing Bloc is a cooperative group of independent and hybrid writers. We work together to provide valuable tools for other writers and to publish quality content for the entertainment of readers.

Find us at www.writingbloc.com, @Writing_Bloc on Twitter, and Writing Bloc on Facebook. Join our community, listen to our podcast, and read our books! We'd love to interact with you.

CPSIA information can be obtained
at www.ICGtesting.com
Printed in the USA
BVHW040736130821
613887BV00009B/316

9 781087 916446